PRAISE FOR
Linda Lael Miller

"One of the hottest romance authors writing today."
—*Romantic Times*

"Linda Lacl Miller creates vibrant characters and stories I defy you to forget."
—Debbie Macomber

"Move over, Anne Rice!"
—*Affaire de Coeur*

"Miller is a master craftswoman at creating unusual story lines [and] charming characters."
—*Rendezvous*

"Ms. Miller has a timeless writing style, and her characters are always vivacious and appealing."
—*Heartstrings Reviews*

A MIDSUMMER DAY'S DREAM

Linda Lael Miller

BERKLEY BOOKS, NEW YORK

THE BERKLEY PUBLISHING GROUP
Published by the Penguin Group
Penguin Group (USA) Inc.
375 Hudson Street, New York, New York 10014, USA
Penguin Group (Canada), 90 Eglinton Avenue East, Suite 700, Toronto, Ontario M4P 2Y3, Canada
(a division of Pearson Penguin Canada Inc.)
Penguin Books Ltd., 80 Strand, London WC2R 0RL, England
Penguin Group Ireland, 25 St. Stephen's Green, Dublin 2, Ireland (a division of Penguin Books Ltd.)
Penguin Group (Australia), 250 Camberwell Road, Camberwell, Victoria 3124, Australia
(a division of Pearson Australia Group Pty. Ltd.)
Penguin Books India Pvt. Ltd., 11 Community Centre, Panchsheel Park, New Delhi—110 017, India
Penguin Group (NZ), Cnr. Airborne and Rosedale Roads, Albany, Auckland 1310, New Zealand
(a division of Pearson New Zealand Ltd.)
Penguin Books (South Africa) (Pty.) Ltd., 24 Sturdee Avenue, Rosebank, Johannesburg 2196,
South Africa

Penguin Books Ltd., Registered Offices: 80 Strand, London WC2R 0RL, England

Previously included in the anthology *With Love*, published by Jove Books, an imprint of The
Berkley Publishing Group. Originally included in the anthology *Timeless*, published by The
Berkley Publishing Group.

This is a work of fiction. Names, characters, places, and incidents either are the product of
the author's imagination or are used fictitiously, and any resemblance to actual persons, living
or dead, business establishments, events, or locales is entirely coincidental.

A MIDSUMMER DAY'S DREAM

A Berkley Book / published by arrangement with the author

PRINTING HISTORY
Berkley edition / March 2006

ISBN: 0-425-21064-2

BERKLEY®
Berkley Books are published by The Berkley Publishing Group,
a division of Penguin Group (USA) Inc.,
375 Hudson Street, New York, New York 10014.
BERKLEY is a registered trademark of Penguin Group (USA) Inc.
The ''B'' design is a trademark belong to Penguin Group (USA) Inc.

PRINTED IN THE UNITED STATES OF AMERICA

10 9 8 7 6 5 4 3 2 1

One

FRANKIE ran one fingertip over the raised letters on her American Express Card—*Francesca Whittier*, it read—while she waited for the clerk to emerge from the back of the small, dusty costume shop at the end of Ainsley Lane.

If she ended up with nothing to wear to the Medieval Fair, an occasion she'd been looking forward to through a long and unusually gray Seattle winter, she would have no one to blame but herself. She might have phoned from the United States weeks ago and reserved something, or had a gown and headdress made by a local seamstress. Instead, she'd been so caught up in running her own small shop that she'd let some important vacation details slide.

For one, she'd counted on her cousin Brian to look after Cinderella's Closet, her store, while she was away, but at the last minute he'd landed a job waiting tables on a cruise ship.

When, she wondered, had a promise stopped being a promise?

Frankie flipped the credit card end over end on the countertop, listening hopefully to the sounds of bustling enterprise coming from the rear of the shop.

"Have you found anything?" she called out, unable to contain her eagerness any longer. There was no discernible reply, just more industrious noises.

Frankie sighed. She had seriously considered canceling her long-awaited trip to England, but in the end she'd taken a deep breath and dialed an employment agency specializing in temporary workers. They'd sent over Mrs. Cullywater, a retired schoolteacher who had once managed her nephew's hamburger franchise.

Mrs. Cullywater was no Lee Iacocca, obviously, but she seemed competent enough; and she was likable. She would hold things together until Frankie returned.

While Frankie was mulling that over, the clerk, a stout man with a monk's halo of graying brown hair and overlapping front teeth, burst into the main part of the shop again. He was carrying a plain muslin dress over one arm, and his expression conveyed both hope and chagrin.

"I'm afraid there's nothing, Miss Whittier, except for this. More seventeenth-century, really, with the lacing up the front of the bodice and all, but it could pass as medieval, I suppose. . . ."

Frankie surveyed the butternut gown in polite dismay, but she had few choices. She could return to London and spend her precious week sightseeing.

She could hide out in her room just down the lane and feel sorry for herself because for the last eighteen months or so, everything had gone wrong for her.

Or, she reflected, she could do what her late-great dad would have recommended—rent the muslin dress, hie herself off to the fair, an event she'd been anticipating ever since she'd read about it in a travel magazine months before, and have the best possible time.

"Will it fit?" she asked, taking the gown from the clerk's hands and holding it up in front of her. She turned toward the full-length mirrors at one side of the shop, but her gaze stopped at the front window.

A man dressed in a wizard's flowing robes and high, pointed hat was hovering there, peering in at her. The shiny threads in the rich purple fabric of his clothing seemed to be spun from moonbeams, and his beard curled grandly down his chest, white laced through with silver.

For a moment, all of time seemed to stop.

Just a guy in a costume, the logical left side of her brain said. *There's a fair going on, remember?*

Frankie blinked, the magician was gone, and the sidewalk was filled with people who were purely ordinary, even in their costumes.

"That must have been the grandest outfit you had in stock," she said, feeling peculiarly off-balance.

The good-natured clerk squinted toward the window. "What? Oh, that knight who just passed? We have lots of those—"

"No," Frankie broke in. "It was Merlin. You must have seen him—he seemed to fill the whole window-pane—"

The clerk frowned. "Didn't see him. Say, are you feeling quite well, miss? You look a mite on the peaky side, if you ask me. It's a cuppa you need."

Frankie yearned for tea, strong, rich, English stuff, of the sort rarely found in the United States, with plenty of milk and sugar. Still, she would wait until she'd returned to her room at the inn, where she could sit down, catch her breath, and sort through her thoughts as she sipped.

"No, thanks," she said in bright tones that sounded brittle even to her.

Nothing unusual had happened, really, and yet Frankie had been moved on some deep level by the sight of the splendid wizard. He was probably just a solicitor from London or a vacationing dentist from Albuquerque, but dressed up in that costume he had seemed the personification of some private myth.

Frankie felt a twinge of the same mysterious enchantment she'd known as a child, when Christmas Eve came around.

She drew a deep breath, pushing her loosely curled blond hair back from her forehead with a slightly damp palm, and indicated the dress. "Will it fit?" she asked again.

The clerk still looked worried, but he smiled. "One size suits all," he said.

Frankie pushed her American Express card toward him. "Fine. Then I'll take it for the whole week of the fair, please," she said.

Approximately five minutes later she left the shop, carrying the muslin dress in a plastic garment bag. The narrow cobbled streets of Grimsley were brimming with happy tourists, most of whom wore medieval clothing.

Frankie hesitated on the narrow sidewalk and peered in every direction, searching for the wizard. She didn't catch so much as a glimpse of him, and her disappointment was out of all proportion to good sense.

She made her way back toward the inn, which, according to a brochure offered at the front desk, had stood on that very spot, in one incarnation or another, for over six hundred years. From Frankie's tiny second-floor room, tucked away at the rear, the ruins of Sunderlin Keep were visible in all their glorious, tragic grandeur.

While gazing at the castle, Frankie thought of its most illustrious inhabitant, a certain Braden Stuart-Ramsey, Duke of Sunderlin. He'd been so important, this fourteenth-century noble, that he had a whole chapter to himself in one of the guidebooks.

Frankie took a moment to indulge in romantic fantasy, imagining the Duke as a handsome, golden-haired knight clad in rich purple and carrying a jeweled sword. Then she smiled and shook the fancy off. True, the whole village resembled a scene from a beautiful fairy tale, but this was Real Life she was dealing with, and she'd keep that in mind.

After spreading the rented dress out on her bed, Frankie called downstairs and asked for raspberry scones and a pot of tea. It was midmorning and she had not taken the time for breakfast before rushing out to the costume shop. Maybe that, along with jet lag, explained her peculiar reaction to the man in the wizard suit.

She was still quite shaken, though at no time had she felt afraid. It was as if she stood on the precipice of a wonderful adventure, her toes curled over the edge, her arms spread in joyous abandon. The very air seemed to vibrate with some crazy magic just beyond the reach of normal sight and hearing.

The tea and scones arrived, brought by a cheerful middle-aged woman straight out of an English novel, with her mobcap, black dress, and pristine white apron. Frankie settled down at the small round table next to the leaded windows to revive herself.

She gazed out through the diamond-shaped panes as she ate. The food did not calm her, as it normally would have; in fact, Frankie was barely aware of taste or texture. The ancient keep held her full attention, and in her admittedly fruitful imagination, she saw guards walking the crumbling parapets. She saw the drawbridge lowered over the moat, pictured a company of horsemen in grand livery riding across.

The yearning to see the castle as it had once been, in the height of its glory days, swelled in Frankie's heart. So strong was her desire that, for a fraction of a moment, she thought she actually caught a glimpse of impenetrable walls and towers, instead of rock piles.

You're imagining things, scoffed a voice in her head. The words didn't come from her overvigilant left-brain, which had a lot to say about almost everything she did, but from Geoffrey Mason, her ex-husband.

She had been divorced from Geoffrey, a handsome and extremely egotistical airline pilot, for almost three years. Frankie, who had been a flight attendant at the time, had given up her job and returned to her hometown of Seattle, where, with a sizable loan from her dad, she'd started Cinderella's Closet.

Miraculously she'd been successful, selling antique jewelry and vintage clothing in her shop, and later recycled designer stuff on consignment as well. She'd even dated a few harmless types.

Still, Frankie had truly loved Geoffrey, and she'd been fragile for a long time, concentrating mainly on survival.

Fate had never seemed crueler than it did the day a year after the divorce, though, when Frankie's dad, her only living relative besides the capricious Brian, had died suddenly in an accident on the freeway.

After that she'd sunk into a sort of functional depression, eating, sleeping, working, doing those things and only those things, in endless succession.

Then she'd read about the yearly week-long medieval fair at Grimsley, just a short bus ride from London, and the idea of going had rolled into her mind and clattered to a stop, like a runaway hubcap. It was just what she needed to jolt herself back on track, she decided, a complete change of scene—even the *illusion* of a different century. Talk about getting away from it all!

Inspired, Frankie had made the decision to stop grieving, to stop hiding, to venture out into the big world again and do something spectacular. Right away she'd been up to her eyeballs in preparations to fly to England and enjoy the fair.

Frankie brought her thoughts sharply back to the here and now and was surprised to find herself giving a little sniffle. Her eyes were filled with tears, and she angrily wiped them away with the heel of her palm.

She shook off the bittersweet reflections that had been quivering on the clear surface of her mind and tidied up the tea tray.

It was time to put the past out of her mind and follow through on a dream.

Frankie set the tray in the hallway, then took off

her white shorts and coral tank top to put on the muslin dress. Her gray eyes widened as she looked at herself in the antique cheval mirror that stood in the corner of the room. Although she saw her own face, her own curly, chin-length blond hair, she also saw a hitherto unrecognized facet of Frankie Whittier. A saucy medieval wench gazed back at her, full of joy, adventure, and mischief.

For a moment the sun-washed dust speckles floating in the room seemed to sparkle, even to make a very faint sound, rather like the tinkle of wind chimes.

Then Geoffrey's influence struck again.

Get a grip, Frankie. You're always living in a fantasy world. That's your trouble.

Frankie smiled and held the muslin skirts wide, as if they were French silk instead, but it was the wench who replied aloud, "Go to hell—and take your opinions with you!"

Frankie laughed, tightened the ribbon laces on the bodice of the dress so that her modest cleavage looked more impressive, then tucked a packet of traveler's checks into her pocket, along with her room key. Her thin platinum watch, a life-goes-on gift from her father after the divorce, was Frankie's only other concession to modern times. She slipped it onto her wrist, where it was hidden by the cuff of her dress, and set out barefoot for the fair.

The sunshine seemed especially bright that day, and the sky was a memorable blue. It seemed to Frankie, as she stopped to purchase a wreath of tiny delicate flowers and trailing ribbons for her hair, that there was magic abroad; sweet, dangerous magic.

She watched the puppeteers for a time and cheered the jousting knights. She laughed and clapped as the mummers put on an impromptu play, then bought a small "dove" pie—which was really made with pheasant—and found a place on the banks of the stream that flowed through the center of the village. There she was, eating her lunch and soaking her bare, dusty feet in the cool water, congratulating herself on what a bold and modern woman she was, when the air around her began to hum.

That excited feeling pooled in her stomach, that Christmas-Eve sensation of old. But this was something much, much bigger.

Frankie leaned back against the trunk of an ancient oak tree and closed her eyes. Not a migraine, she thought, for she hadn't had one of her headaches since before Geoffrey left her. Too young for a stroke. And why do I feel so happy?

The humming sound grew to a roar, and Frankie waited. Maybe she was having a nervous breakdown or some kind of manic episode. That would explain her exhilaration—wouldn't it?

When she opened her eyes again, she was stunned to see that the world had altered itself during those tumultuous seconds just past.

The stream was wider and deeper, and there was a wooden bridge where the stone one had stood before. The grass she sat upon was fragrantly verdant and quite untrampled. The village itself stood at a distance, and the brick buildings had been replaced by cottages and huts of wattle and daub, with thatched roofs. Though there were people about as before, they weren't the *same* people. Their clothing was rustic, rougher-looking than before, and most of them had bad skin and even worse teeth.

But what drew Frankie's attention was the spectacle of Sunderlin Keep.

The castle loomed whole and sturdy and magnificent against the soft blue of the English sky. The drawbridge looked sturdy, and there was a moat, full of murky water.

Frankie stared in amazement, blinked, and stared again. The scene did not fade.

She climbed unsteadily to her feet, crumbling the pie in a nervous grip, and pressed her back to the oak tree. It too was different, a younger tree, hardly more than a sapling, and flexible.

One of the villagers pointed at her and spoke to a colleague, and some sort of stir began. Frankie was both terrified and intrigued as mummers and jugglers, merchants and minor nobles all stopped to stare.

The way they were acting, *she* might have been the hallucination, and not them. Fleetingly she wondered again if she was experiencing some kind of individual myth, a colorful gift from her subconscious mind, fraught with meaning.

The crowd began to press around her, pointing and gaping. The smell of them, coupled with the wild confusion she was feeling, nearly overwhelmed Frankie. They were babbling, questioning, but their language was like the Chaucer stuff she remembered from high school, and she could comprehend only a word here and there.

Just when Frankie thought her knees were sure to give out, that she would drop helpless to the ground, someone came pushing through the crowd, a tall, broad-shouldered someone with golden-brown hair and eyes of the same intriguing color. He wore gray leggings, leather shoes, and a purple tunic with a complicated image of a lion embroidered on the front. At his side swung a sword that might have been a cousin to Excalibur.

Frankie stared up into those sharply intelligent brown eyes, at the same time reaching behind her to clutch the supple oak with both hands, in an effort to stay on her feet.

"I don't know how you people managed to make this all seem so real," she blurted out, her tongue driven by nervousness rather than wisdom, "but I'm impressed."

The towering vision before her frowned, and his brow furrowed slightly. The crowd around them began to murmur again, and he stilled them with a gesture of one hand and a brusque, "Silence!"

One disjointed moment hobbled by before Frankie realized that he'd spoken in modern vernacular. She felt an odd certainty that her deeper mind was translating his Old English into words she could understand.

She put out one hand. "Hello, there," she said, her voice shaking only slightly. "I'm Francesca Whittier."

The giant looked at her hand, then gazed into her eyes for what seemed like a long time before grasping her fingers in greeting.

Frankie came close to fainting again, this time because his grip was so tight. "And you are—?" she managed to squeak.

He bowed slightly. "I am Braden Stuart-Ramsey, Duke of Sunderlin," he said. He ran his impudent gaze over her rented muslin dress. "Are your favors for hire? You look suitable for an afternoon's entertainment."

Frankie felt as though she'd been caught between

two revolving doors, both turning in opposite directions. She was awestruck on the one hand, not only by the situation but by the Duke's title. On the other hand, she was outraged at his blatant presumption.

Her dignity prevailed. "You're not anything like I imagined you to be from what I read in the guidebooks. Furthermore, you will have to look elsewhere for your afternoon's amusements, I'm afraid, because I don't sing or dance."

The Duke threw back his head and laughed, and the rich, masculine abandon of the sound stirred Frankie on a level of her being she had not been aware of before. "Take her to the keep," he said to someone standing just outside the hazy edges of Frankie's vision.

"But, Your Grace—"

"Now," Sunderlin interrupted.

She felt someone grasp her arm as the Duke turned and walked away, parting the crowd like the waters of the Red Sea as he passed.

"Now, just a moment, you," Frankie protested. She took a step away from the tree. When she did, the sky did a quick spin, her stomach jumped, and then the ground seemed to rush toward her.

BRADEN paused when she dared to challenge him, turned, and saw the wench crumpled in the summer grass. No one came forward to offer her aid, and from the way all the villagers hung back, staring and pointing, it was plain they were afraid of her. Damn them and their incessant superstitions; their lives were ruled by fearful imaginings of all sorts.

He went back, crouched, and lifted her into his arms. She felt strong and at the same time fragile, and something tugged at Braden's gut, deep down. Reaching his horse, he swung up onto the gelding's back, hauling his captive along with him.

A grin lifted one corner of his mouth as she opened her stone-gray eyes, looked up at him, sighed, and then sank against his chest again.

Braden turned his mount toward Sunderlin Keep and the drawbridge, reflecting as he rode, leaving the midsummer fair behind. She was a spectacular creature, this insensible wench in his arms, unusually fine and strong, clearly a misfit. He empathized with the loneliness of that, having always felt strangely misplaced in the world himself.

The villagers surely thought this woman was an angel, or a splendid witch.

She sighed again, looking up at him in a guileless way, and said, "If you're wondering why I'm not kicking and screaming right now, it's because I know I'm dreaming this. You aren't real—none of this is real—it's probably all part of some weird sexual fantasy."

Braden frowned. What an odd pronouncement. "Sexual fantasy"? Why would anyone indulge in such fancies when the real experience was so easily had?

He thought again of what the villagers were probably saying by now, and shook his head. It could not be denied, however, that this wench was different. She was bigger and stronger than any woman he'd ever seen—God's breath but she felt heavy on his arm, even though she was sleekly made—and her skin and teeth *were* uncommonly good. Still, Braden reasoned, he himself was of rare good health and sturdy construction, and he was certainly neither angel nor warlock.

"What," he began as they crossed the drawbridge, the hooves of his charger making a rhythmic sound on the wood, "are you blathering about?"

She took a deep breath, wiping aside the two bright ribbons that dangled across her face from the halo of flowers, now sitting askew on her head. "Well," she replied, "it's not something I can explain easily. I've always had a thing for knights and castles, and I played Guinevere in our high school production of *Camelot*—"

They passed beneath the points of the iron portcullis and into the lower bailey. "Guinevere?" Braden asked, somewhat shortly. He'd heard the legends of King Arthur as a child, and loved them, but he couldn't see what they had to do with the afternoon's events. "I thought you said you were called Francesca."

She smiled, and the effect was startling; rather like sunlight flashing suddenly upon very clear water. Once again he felt a lurching sensation, much like the time in his boyhood when he'd nearly toppled off a cliff and a companion had caught hold of his tunic just in time to pull him back. "My friends call me Frankie," she said.

Braden couldn't help smiling back, even though he didn't approve of a woman having such a name— even if she was a lightskirt, selling her favors at a country fair. "Frankie" was better suited to a lad; to him, she would always be "Francesca."

Always? The word stretched through Braden's mind like a vine gone wild, making him distinctly uncomfortable.

"Are you traveling with the mummers or the puppeteers?" he asked. "I haven't seen you before."

She laughed, and the sound quivered in his heart

like a lance, at once painful and sweet. "You know, it's just like me to have a fantasy where the man who is going to ravish me turns out to be a nice guy. You are nice, aren't you?"

He was baffled again, and at no behest from him, his arm tightened slightly around her. "I don't know," he replied thoughtfully. "No one has ever described me that way as far as I know." Braden felt his neck reddening, drew back on the reins, and swung one muscular leg over the saddle horn, at the same time lowering Francesca to the ground. "Furthermore," he said, "I've never *ravished* a woman in my life. They've always come to my bed quite willingly."

Francesca's flawless cheeks turned pink, and the gray eyes sparked. "Fantasy or no fantasy, buddy," she replied, "I'm not going to your bed, period. Willingly or otherwise."

Braden dismounted. "We'll see," he said. He tossed the reins to a stable boy and gripped Francesca's arm with his other hand, propelling her up the slope toward the keep.

Two

SOLICITOUSLY the Duke straightened the berib-
boned floral wreath Frankie had bought earlier, in
the real world. Then, with an air of amused ceremony, he squired her under a high archway and into
the keep's Great Hall.

There were rushes on the floor, and knights
lounged at long trestle tables, playing dice and arm
wrestling. There was no hearth or chimney but instead a huge firepit in the center of the hall. Smoke
meandered toward a large round hole in the roof,
turning the air acrid before disappearing into the
sky.

Frankie coughed, blinking because her eyes burned
and because she couldn't believe what she was seeing.
Surely this was the most elaborate hallucination anyone
had ever had, without taking drugs first.

She rubbed her right temple nervously. Maybe the
scones she'd had at the inn that morning had been

laced with something. Or perhaps someone had slipped her a mickey at the fair.

Both scenarios seemed unlikely, but so did finding herself in a place she'd only read about, a time centuries in the past. Just then, not much of anything was making sense to Frankie—including the staggering and surely ill-advised attraction she felt toward the Duke.

The men-at-arms looked up from their mugs and games to leer at Frankie in earnest, but one quelling glance from the Duke made them all subside again.

"What year is this?" Frankie asked, squinting up at Sunderlin's daunting profile as he double-stepped her over the rushes toward a wide stone stairway lined with unlit torches.

He looked down at her and frowned, but he didn't slacken his pace. "It is the year of our Lord thirteen hundred and sixty-seven," he answered. "Where have you been that you had to ask such a question? Even in nunneries, they mark the passage of time."

Frankie's head was spinning, and she felt a peculiar mix of desire and utter terror. They were taking the stairs at a good clip; evidently, this fantasy was going to reach its dramatic crescendo soon.

"If I told you where I'd been, you'd never believe me," she replied. "Suffice it to say, it wasn't a 'nunnery,' as you put it." She dug in her heels, or tried to, but the Duke just kept walking. "Wait a second! Could we just stop and talk, please? I mean, I know this is all a production of my subconscious mind, starring me, with a guest appearance by you, but I'm not ready to play out the big scene."

Sunderlin finally halted, square in the middle of the upper hallway, and stared at Frankie as if completely confounded. It was all so real—the dank stone walls of the castle, the burnt-pitch smell of the torches, the remarkable muscular man standing beside her. She marveled at the power of the human imagination; clearly, her yearnings for adventure and romance had run much deeper than she'd ever guessed. Now her mind was producing the whole dream like some elaborate play, though she must remember that it was all taking place inside her head.

"What in the name of God are you talking about?" he demanded. Even in his consternation, the Duke exuded self-confidence and personal strength.

Frankie reached out and pressed one palm to the cold rock wall, to steady herself. She was ready to wake up now, ready to go home to Kansas, so to speak, and yet the idea of never seeing Sunderlin again struck a resonant note of sorrow in her heart. It was a sensation she couldn't have explained, as mystical as the experience in general.

"I don't feel so good," she said.

Sunderlin bent his knees and peered into her face, which was probably quite pale by then. "You don't have the plague, I hope," he replied.

Frankie could only shake her head.

"Here, then, you're probably starving, and it's plain that you've come from some far place." He lifted her into his arms again, just as he had at the fair, when she'd been surrounded by curious villagers. "I'll send for some food and wine, and when you've had a rest, I'll bed you."

Frankie's temper flared, even though she knew she was only dreaming. "That's very generous of you, my lord," she said tartly. Sunderlin carried her into yet another large, drafty chamber and dumped her onto a bed roughly the size of her whole apartment back home. "Now, what on earth does *this* symbolize?" she muttered, distracted for a moment, as she patted the thick feather mattress with both hands.

"Enough of your strange chatter," Sunderlin growled, bending over her and forcing her backward until she was lying flat. His arms were like stone pillars on either side of her as he leaned on the bed. "God's kneecaps, woman, the villagers are sure to think you're either a witch or an angel. There's something very different about you, and to their minds, anyone who is different is dangerous. If they decide you're a sorceress, they might very well stone you or burn you at the stake!"

Frankie was completely undone, but not by the delusion she was having or even by the prospect of being executed for sorcery. No, it was the proximity of Braden Stuart-Ramsey, Duke of Sunderlin, that was making her so wildly nervous.

She reached up, with a trembling hand, to touch his tanned, clean-shaven face. "You seem so real, so solid."

He made an exasperated sound, then leaned closer still and brushed his lips across hers. His mouth felt soft and warm, and a hot shiver rushed through Frankie's system.

"I am definitely 'real,'" Sunderlin said, his voice hoarse. Then, just when Frankie wanted the fantasy to continue, he pushed himself away from her and stood straight beside the bed. Never taking his eyes from hers, he unbuckled his sword belt and laid it aside, weapon and all. "Who are you, Francesca?" he asked. "Where did you come from?"

Frankie knew she should have bounded off that bed immediately—everything she believed as a modern, right-thinking female demanded it—but she was possessed of an odd lethargy. She yawned. "This is not going to compute," she said, "but since you insist, here goes. My name is Francesca Whittier, and I'm from the United States."

Sunderlin pulled his tunic off over the top of his head, revealing a broad, hairy chest and powerful shoulders. His glorious caramel-colored hair was rumpled by the process. "The United States?" he asked, giving a braided bellpull a hard wrench and then reaching for a ewer of water sitting on a nearby table. "I've never heard of that place. Where is it?"

"On the other side of the Atlantic Ocean," Frankie said, watching him. As hallucinations went, the Duke of Sunderlin was downright delicious. "At this point you could only describe it as—underdeveloped."

A servant entered the room, probably in reply to Sunderlin's yank on the bellpull, a bow-legged little man in leggings and a tunic that looked as though it might have been made of especially coarse burlap.

The Duke spoke to him in an undertone, and he disappeared again. Even though the servant had not so much as glanced in Frankie's direction, his curiosity had been palpable.

"Mordag will bring you bread and wine," Sunderlin said. He'd washed his face and upper body and was now drying himself with his discarded tunic. "As I said, you may eat and sleep for a reasonable time. Then you and I will work out an agreement."

Frankie felt her cheeks turn hot again. "I very much appreciate your hospitality," she said in measured tones. "However, there's no need for us to 'work out an agreement.' As I told you before, I am not a prostitute."

Sunderlin's white teeth flashed in a grin so lethal it should have been registered somewhere. He folded his arms, which Frankie now noticed were scarred in places, and tilted his magnificent head to one side. "I see," he teased. "Then you must be a lady—one who's fallen upon unfortunate circumstances." He sketched a deep bow, and Frankie was flushed with fury, knowing he was mocking her.

At last she found the strength to scramble into a sitting position; not an easy task, since the mattress was so deep and soft. "I'd have *been* a lady if I'd gotten to the costume shop on time," she blurted.

"What?" he asked, frowning again.

"Never mind!" Frankie floundered around on the mattress for a while, making no progress. She finally turned over onto her belly and wriggled until she reached the side, where she swung her legs over and stood. "My point is," she went on, while Sunderlin stood grinning at her, "you shouldn't assume that I'm a loose woman just because of my clothes!"

Sunderlin approached, hooked one finger through the laces that held Frankie's bodice together. Underneath, she was wearing only a thin camisole of sand-washed silk. "Witch or angel," he said, his voice low and throaty, "you are fascinating."

Frankie swallowed and retreated a step. "Don't touch me," she said, without conviction.

Sunderlin reached out and pulled her against him. "Fascinating," he repeated.

She stiffened. "Are you planning to force me?" she demanded. "Because if you are, I'm warning you, I'll knee you where it hurts, and I'll scream my head off, too. Your reputation will be completely ruined!"

He threw back his head and laughed, and when he looked into her eyes again, a moment later, she saw kindness in his gaze, along with desire and amusement. "My reputation will be ruined," he corrected, "if the servants do not hear you crying out in passion." Sunderlin paused, sighed philosophically. "Didn't I tell you before, little witch? I have never in my life taken a woman who did not want my attentions." He held her loosely, his arms linked behind the small of her back, and bent to kiss the pulse point at the base of her throat.

Frankie felt faint. "Good," she replied when she could manage to speak. "I'm—I'm glad."

Sunderlin touched her breast, very gently, his thumb passing over one muslin-covered nipple and causing it to blossom. "Of course," he went on, idly entangling a finger in the laces that held her bodice closed, "I have no doubt that I can rouse a fever in you."

His arrogance was like a snowball in the face, and Frankie jerked back out of his arms just as the servant reappeared, carrying a tray. She turned away, embarrassed, and when she looked in Sunderlin's direction again, he had pulled on a clean tunic and the servant was gone.

"Refresh yourself," the Duke commanded, pausing in front of a looking glass to run splayed fingers through his hair. "I will return later." He paused as Frankie inspected the items on the tray. "Just in case you're thinking of escaping," he added, in grave tones, "don't. My men would find you before sunset, and honor would require that I punish you."

Frankie was too confused and scared to think about escape just then, but she meant to entertain the notion later, when she'd had a little time to gather her wits. She sketched a curtsy every bit as mocking as his bow had been earlier. "Your word is my command, O Pompous and Arrogant One," she said. Then she took a piece of dark bread from the trencher and examined it for weevils and other moving violations.

Sunderlin only grinned, strapped on Excalibur again, and walked out of the massive room, leaving Frankie quite alone.

She bit into the bread and reached for a brass bottle, which contained a bitter and very potent red wine. Normally, Frankie didn't drink, but on that day all the other rules of the universe seemed to be suspended—why not that one?

Having eaten, and consumed the wine, Frankie began to feel light-headed and sleepy again. Good, she thought. I'll wake up in my bed at the Grimsley Inn, or even back in Seattle, in my apartment, and all this will be over. A dream and nothing more.

As before, the thought of leaving Sunderlin left her strangely bereft, and close to tears.

She sniffled once as she stretched out on the featherbed.

Hours later she awakened to the same room, the same stone walls, and her shock was exceeded only by her relief. The dream or delusion had not yet ended, and she was glad, though she couldn't have offered a rational explanation for her attitude. Luckily, no one was asking for one.

"Mr. Stuart-Ramsey?" she called tentatively. "My lord?"

There was no response, but in the distance she heard the sounds of raucous male laughter and the music of some sort of pipe, as well as a stringed instrument or two. Frankie rolled to the side of the bed and struggled to her feet, smoothing her hair and her muslin skirts.

By the light of the moon, which came in through narrow windows empty of glass, Frankie found the bellpull, stared at it for a few moments, and then gripped the cord in both hands and gave it a good jerk.

The spindly servant appeared almost instantly, and Frankie wondered if the poor man was compelled to work at night as well as during the day. He carried a flickering candle, which he used to light oil lamps set around the room.

"You may tell the Duke that I will see him now," Frankie announced, with great dignity. Never mind that it was mostly pretense; she *sounded* sure of herself even if she wasn't.

Mordag merely looked at her in bewilderment and something like awe. His Adam's apple traveled the length of his scrawny, unwashed neck as he stood there, apparently at a complete loss to understand her instructions.

She drew a deep breath and very patiently began again. "I said—"

"He won't speak to you," a familiar voice interrupted. "He probably fears you'll either cast a spell over him or strike him dead for some secret sin."

Frankie turned and saw Sunderlin standing in the doorway. He said something unintelligible to Mordag, and the servant rushed from the room, plainly eager to be gone.

"Couldn't you just tell these people that I'm an ordinary woman?" she asked, exasperated.

Sunderlin smiled and ran his gaze over her in a leisurely way. "They wouldn't believe me," he replied after a moment's reflection. "And why should they? It's plain to any man with eyes that you're no 'ordinary woman.' "

Frankie felt dizzying confusion, as well as a terrible attraction to this strange and powerful man. She averted her eyes for a moment, wondering that a mere delusion, a figment of her imagination, could stir her the way Sunderlin did.

"Have you rested?" the Duke asked when she failed to continue the conversation, sitting down at a rough-hewn table near the bed and putting his feet up.

Unconsciously Frankie tightened the laces on her rented dress. "Yes," she said. "If you would just take me to a hotel now, I would appreciate it very much."

"Take you where?"

"An inn," Frankie said in frustration. "A tavern—"

Sunderlin swung his powerful legs down from the tabletop and rose to his feet in a graceful surge of rage. "You would prefer such a place to my bed?" he demanded, breathing the words more than speaking them.

Frankie figured since this was a fantasy, she might as well be honest. "No," she said. "I guess not."

He approached her slowly. "You are a beautiful and very complicated creature," he said. "And you will be even lovelier in the throes of pleasure. Let me show you, Francesca." Sunderlin untied the laces at the bodice of her dress, and she did nothing to stop him.

"If—if I want you to stop—then—?"

"Then I shall stop," the Duke said.

Frankie closed her eyes as she felt the dress part, felt the cool night air spread over her breasts, causing the nipples to jut against the thin silk of her camisole.

"Lovely," Sunderlin said. He smoothed the dress down over her shoulders with excruciating gentleness, then removed the camisole, too. "So lovely."

Frankie trembled, afraid to meet his gaze even

though his words and his tone held quiet reverence.
He made her feel like a fallen goddess, too beautiful
to be real.

"Look at me," the Duke commanded as he caressed first one breast and then the other. His touch
had the weight of a moonbeam, the fierce heat of a
newly spawned star.

She could not resist the order, could not move
away or lift a hand to stop his sweet plundering. She
met his eyes, entranced.

"What are you?" he asked in a raspy voice. "Tell
me now, be you angel or witch?"

Frankie gave a long, quivering sigh as he fondled
an eager nipple. "This is some fantasy," she said.
"Wow."

Sunderlin bent, took the morsel he'd been caressing into his mouth, and suckled, wringing a cry of
startled pleasure from Frankie's lips.

"Answer me," he said when he'd raised his head
again.

Frankie wanted to press him back to her bosom,
to nourish him, to set his senses ablaze as he had
hers. "I'm whatever you want me to be," she replied,
and she was rewarded by a low groan and the con-
quest of her other breast.

God only knew what would have happened if the
clanging sound of metal striking stone hadn't
sounded from the passage outside Sunderlin's chamber, along with a good-natured and exuberant male
voice.

"Braden!" the visitor called as the Duke swore
and Frankie dived for the shadowy end of the chamber, struggling to right her dress. The clang sounded
again, louder and closer. "Are you in there wench-
ing, like Mordag says?"

Frankie heard Sunderlin swear and peered out of the gloom, holding the bodice of her dress closed, her breathing still fast and very shallow. A handsome man, younger than the Duke and much darker in coloring, swaggered into the room, sheathing his sword as he entered. Apparently, it had been the blade of that weapon that Frankie had heard striking the stone walls.

Sunderlin shrugged, adjusting his tunic. "Alaric," he greeted the other man, and there was an undercurrent of humor flowing beneath his irritation. "I thought you were in London Town, pandering at court."

Alaric laughed, ignoring the Duke's jibe and looking around with an expression of impudent curiosity. "Come now, Brother, where is she? I must see the creature or perish of wondering. Mordag says she's too beautiful and too perfect to be a human woman."

"Mordag talks too much," Sunderlin answered. He went to a side table, though it couldn't have been plainer that he didn't welcome company, and poured wine into two ornate silver chalices. "Show yourself, Francesca, or my brother will seek you out. He's just brazen enough to do it."

Frankie would have preferred to remain in the shadows, since she'd never found her camisole and, even though she'd pulled up her dress and tied the laces, there was still a lot of skin showing through. She came out of her hiding place anyway, her arms crossed demurely across her chest.

Alaric was definitely a new development, and she wondered where he fit into her fantasy.

He studied her with dark, shrewd eyes. Clearly, Alaric had the same forthright, supremely confident nature as his brother. Frankie was both relieved and puzzled to realize that she understood him clearly, as she did Braden.

"Neither angel nor witch," he said in a speculative tone, the hint of a smile lifting one corner of his mouth. "No, Brother, this is surely a wood nymph, or a mermaid weary of the sea."

What a line, Frankie thought, but she liked Alaric. It would have been impossible not to, for he was charming. She smiled as he took her hand and lightly kissed her knuckles. Out of the corner of her eye, she saw Sunderlin frowning ominously.

"Do not become too enchanted," he warned in a quiet voice. "Nymph or mermaid, angel or witch, Francesca is mine."

Frankie's proud heart pumped hot crimson color into her cheeks. "Unlike your favorite horse and your hunting dogs," she said, "I am not 'yours'! I'm my own."

Sunderlin's jaw tightened, and Alaric chuckled, obviously amused by his brother's annoyance. "Such a quick tongue," he said.

" 'How sharper than a serpent's tooth,' " Frankie quoted, getting into the spirit of things. She might as well enjoy this delusion to the hilt; there was no telling when or if she'd be able to work up another one like it.

"That's very good," said Alaric, waggling an index finger. "Someone should write it down."

"Someone will, someday," Frankie assured him.

Sunderlin narrowed his eyes again. "Witch talk," he said. "Have you no sense at all?"

The words stung. "Yes," Frankie snapped. "I also have a sense of humor—a claim *you* certainly can't make!"

"Sparks!" Alaric cried, spreading his arms in a gesture of expansive delight. "The air is blue with them!"

"Silence!" Sunderlin boomed, but it was Frankie he was glowering at, not his brother.

"In your dreams," Frankie answered, folding her arms and lifting her chin. Okay, so she was having a fantasy. Okay, so it was probably a *sexual* fantasy. That didn't mean she was going to let a man push her around, no matter how attractive she found him.

Alaric laughed again, bracing himself against a table edge with both hands. "At last," he said. "A woman who doesn't tremble before you like a blade of grass in a high wind. Brother, your fate is sealed. You are doomed. Congratulations!"

"Out," Sunderlin said. His gaze rested on the pulse point at the base of Frankie's throat, or so it seemed to her, but there was no doubt that he was addressing Alaric.

The younger brother bowed, but his good spirits were as evident as before. "As you wish," he said graciously. "Never fear, Braden. I will carry the news of your conquering to every part of England."

At last Sunderlin's stare shifted from Frankie to his sibling, and she let out an involuntary sigh of relief. The expression on the Duke's face could only have been called ferocious. "We will speak privately," he said to Alaric. "Now."

Frankie watched, a little nettled that she'd been forgotten so easily, as both men left the chamber.

Three

IT was that night, while she waited in vain in Sunderlin's bedchamber, alternately cursing Braden and praying for his return, that Frankie started to accept the possibility that the experience she was having was not a flight of fancy at all, but some new facet of reality.

A delusion, she reasoned as she lay beneath the covers on Braden's bed, clad only in her silk camisole and tap pants, would surely have faded by this time. Furthermore, while no sensible person would ever have described Frankie as a hardheaded realist, she wasn't given to wild imaginings, either. She wasn't insane, and her surroundings were simply too solid for a hallucination. The only other explanation was that she had slipped through some unseen doorway, into another time.

How could such a thing happen? Frankie had no answers, only questions. What seemed most remarkable to her was her own resilience—nervous break-downs are made of such stuff as she was experiencing, and yet she had a sense of well-being and belonging now that had eluded her since childhood.

The first pink light of dawn was just creeping across the stone floor when Braden reappeared, looking rumpled and somewhat bleary-eyed.

Frankie sat bolt upright in bed, heedless of her near-naked state, furious jealousy flowing through her. Even with Geoffrey, she had never felt any emotion so intense. "Where have you been?" she demanded.

To her infinite exasperation, Braden grinned. "Not with a wench," he replied, "so calm yourself." He went to a table uncomfortably near the bed and poured water from a ewer into a waiting basin. He made a great production of stripping off his tunic and washing.

That done, he removed his soft leather shoes and woolen leggings as well. He loomed beside the bed, gloriously naked and utterly without self-consciousness.

Frankie's arousal was complete, and unbidden, and she was mortified by it. Blushing, she wriggled down under the bedclothes.

Braden promptly tossed back the thick fur coverings and surveyed her. "Such a strange manner of dress," he said, clearly confounded by her lingerie. "Still, I imagine you're a regular woman under-neath."

Frankie's cheeks burned. She was two women, all of a sudden—one sensible and modest, one wanting nothing so much as to thrash beneath this man in noisy abandon. "Why is this happening?" she mur-mured. "Why me?"

The Duke bent over her, hooked his big thumbs

under the waistband of Frankie's tap pants, and slid them deftly down over her thighs. She could only watch, stunned at the depths of her own feminine need, as he frowned, apparently more interested in watching the elastic stretch when he pulled, then snap back into place.

Finally he tossed the tap pants aside and looked at Frankie with a possessiveness and hunger that made her blood heat. With one hand he parted her thighs; with the other he tugged upward on her camisole.

Frankie closed her eyes and groaned softly as Braden's fingers claimed the most private part of her. It did no good, telling herself that this was no fantasy after all, that what was happening was real and would have its consequences. This was more than a mere encounter; Frankie felt as though she and Braden had been drawn together from separate parts of the universe.

She thrilled to his weight and warmth as he stretched out beside her. He bent his head to nibble at her breasts, one and then the other, all the while gently caressing her most feminine place.

He made a low, sighlike sound as Frankie began to twist and writhe under his attentions. Although she had thought she'd known pleasure before, with Geoffrey, the fitful realization came to her that she had instead been entirely innocent until this man, Braden Stuart-Ramsey, Duke of Sunderlin, touched her.

Braden nipped lightly at Frankie's nipple while at the same moment plunging his fingers deep inside her, and she arched her back and gave a strangled, joyous cry of welcome.

"Braden," she pleaded, not precisely sure what she

was begging for, clutching at his bare shoulders with both hands. "Oh, dear God—Braden—"

He raised his head from her breast to look straight into her eyes. "This is what you were made for," he said, "and what I was made for. No, no—don't close your eyes, witch. Let me see your magic."

Frankie was practically out of her mind with need by that point, and Braden showed her no quarter. While his thumb made an endless, tantalizing circle, his fingers alternately teased and conquered.

She began to toss her head from side to side on the pillow while the incomprehensible ecstasy carried her higher and higher. Braden was choreographing her every move, and he would not let her look away, yet she had never known a greater sense of freedom. She was, in those fiery moments, more truly herself than she had ever been.

Frankie arched high off the mattress, a long, high, keening cry spilling from her throat as wild spasms of pleasure seized her. Again and again, her body buckled in fierce release, and Braden held her entranced the whole time, not only physically, but emotionally as well.

When at last she was sated, and she lay breathless and quivering, her flesh moist from her exertions, Braden caressed her, all over, with his big, gentle hands. He spoke soothingly and kissed places that still trembled with the aftershocks of cataclysmic pleasure, and then he held her. The holding, in its way, was as fulfilling as her repeated climaxes had been.

Frankie could not have said how much time had passed by the time Braden mounted her; she was only half-conscious, lost in bliss.

Braden took her wrists in his hands, frowning a

little when he felt the band of her watch but not pausing to examine it, and raised her arms high over her head so that his body lay flush with hers.

"As I told you," he said, kissing her jaw as he spoke, "I have never taken a woman against her will. I want to be part of you, Francesca, to make you a part of me. Will you allow that?"

She whimpered softly, sleepily, feeling her nipples harden against his hairy chest and her feminine passage expand to receive him. "Please," she said, opening her legs. She was still intoxicated, and sleep beckoned seductively. "But—you will forgive me, won't you—if I drift off—?"

He chuckled. "You will be wide wake in a moment, witch," he said. "What happened before was only a preparation for this."

Truer words had never been spoken.

Frankie's heavy eyelids flew up as Braden entered her in one strong stroke, arousing her sated body all over again, bringing every nerve ending to frantic awareness.

Braden glided in and out of her a few times, still holding her wrists above her head, though gently, watching her face as though he found every changing expression fascinating. He was a modern lover, ahead of his violent, uncaring time.

When he knew she was wild with need, he withdrew and whispered raspily, "Tell me, beautiful Francesca—are you angel or witch?"

"Witch," she half-sobbed, and Braden lunged deep into her, covering her mouth with his own in the same instant and swallowing her shouts of passion.

It was dizzying, like riding some cosmic roller coaster. Every moment, every nuance had to be experienced; there was no going back.

Until that morning Frankie had considered herself a knowledgeable woman. Admittedly, her past was unspectacular when it came to romance; she'd been intimate with Geoffrey and before him, a guy she'd dated in high school and college. She'd been aroused and, yes, satisfied, in a sweetly innocuous sort of way.

Now the Duke of Sunderlin, a man who might not even exist, had shown her that there were whole universes yet to be discovered and explored. He'd turned her inside out and outside in, and somehow, in a way she couldn't define, he'd given her a totally new sense of herself.

Braden held her for a long time, like before, then rose whistling from the bed to don a fresh tunic and woolen leggings. "I have things to attend to today," he said, pausing to pat Frankie solicitously on the bottom. "You can explore the keep if you want, and the grounds, too. Just don't wander into the village."

Frankie sat up, her sense of challenge stirred. "Why not?"

Braden shrugged. "Do as you wish, then. Be advised, though, that the villagers are saying you appeared out of nowhere—one moment, nothing, the next, there you were. Half of them want to declare you a saint and worship you accordingly, and the others lean toward roasting you on a spit, like a pig."

Frankie's eyes went wide, and her throat constricted as she imagined a martyr's death. "I'm scared!"

He kissed the tip of her nose. "Wise woman. I don't suppose I have to tell you that from the beginning, saints have fared even worse than witches. People can't bear the contrast, you see, between what they are and what they believe they should be."

"Thanks for trying to reassure me," Frankie

snapped as Braden straightened and began strapping on his sword belt.

Braden grinned. "You're most welcome, milady. I'll have Mordag bring you one of my sister's gowns, as well as some breakfast."

Frankie brightened at the prospect of female companionship. "You have a sister, then. I would enjoy meeting her."

Braden's expression had turned stony, all in the space of a few moments. "That is impossible," he said. Then, without further explanation, he turned and walked out of the chamber, leaving Frankie alone.

True to his word, however, Braden sent Mordag with an underskirt and kirtle of the softest blue wool, brown bread and spotted pears for breakfast, and a ewer of clean water for washing.

Within half an hour Frankie had eaten, given herself a bath of sorts, and gotten dressed. The underskirt and kirtle were delightful; just what she'd hoped to find in the costume shop, the morning after her arrival in England.

Frankie stopped on the stone stairway, pressing one hand to the cold wall as if to test its substance. Odd, but her "memories" of a world six centuries in the future seemed to be fading, like a random dream.

It was real, she told herself, as real as this. Seattle, the inn, the costume shop, all of it was real. I mustn't forget.

She proceeded, after a moment, keeping to the rear passageways. She paused and hid in the shadows when she heard voices, not wanting to encounter superstitious servants or men-at-arms who might well consider her fair game.

Alas, Frankie had little or no experience at sneaking out of castles. She had almost gained the kitchen, and was looking back over one shoulder to make sure no one was following her, when she collided hard with Alaric.

He steadied her by gripping her shoulders. "Please, lovely one," he pleaded in a teasing voice, "tell me you've found the strength of soul to spurn my legendary brother."

Frankie was uneasy, even though Alaric's smile was ready and his touch was gentle. She sensed that he harbored some dangerous fury behind those bright, mirthful eyes. She shook her head. "Sorry," she responded, somewhat gravely. "I've never met anyone like Braden, and I rather enjoy his company."

That was certainly an understatement, she thought, as memories of just how intensely she'd enjoyed the Duke's company filled her mind. She was grateful for the dim light of the hallway, not wanting Alaric to see her blush.

For a fraction of a moment, a time so brief that Frankie would always wonder if she'd imagined it, Alaric's grasp on her shoulders tightened. His dazzling grin seemed slightly brittle as he released her.

"You shouldn't be wandering through the keep alone, milady," he said with a courtly bow of his head. "I'm surprised Braden allowed such a breach, as a matter of fact." Alaric paused, shrugged. "He leaves me no choice but to uphold the family honor by escorting you myself."

Frankie was still troubled by something in Alaric's manner, but she had to agree that it was safer to have a companion. "I'm happy to know that chivalry is not dead after all," she said.

They crossed the kitchen, a massive room empty except for two great hounds that lay sleeping on the hearth. When Alaric led her into a grassy sideyard, where sunlight played golden, like visible music, Frankie's spirits rose a notch.

Like all natives of Seattle, Frankie was reverently fond of sunshine. She raised her face to the light and spent a moment just soaking up the glorious stuff. When she opened her eyes, Alaric was smiling at her.

"I'm told that you arrived—er—quite suddenly yesterday, at the village fair," he said. "Is that true?"

Frankie lifted the skirts of her cloud-soft woolen dress and set off across the grass, headed for a copse of trees she'd spotted earlier, from Braden's window. She wondered if the branches of the maple were sturdy enough to support her, and if she'd be able to see over the castle wall if she climbed high.

"Of course not," she lied blithely, sensing that it would not be wise to tell Alaric what had really happened. "I arrived with a mummers' troupe and simply took my place in the crowd without being noticed."

Alaric kept up, taking long strides. His build was similar to Braden's, except that he was smaller, and his bone structure seemed fragile by comparison. "Of course I wouldn't think of questioning your word, milady, but it's hard to imagine you passing unnoticed anywhere. You seem to glow, and there's a knowingness in your manner, as if you might be privy to secrets the rest of us could never grasp."

They passed through tall grass, moving between stone outbuildings that looked deserted, while Frankie considered her reply. She saw the maple trees up ahead, beckoning, offering her solace in their fragrant green leaves.

In the end she decided to respond by countering

with a question. "What does it matter where I came from? Surely you don't believe that superstitious rot about my being a witch or an angel."

Frankie thought she saw a muscle tighten in Alaric's jaw, though she couldn't be certain. "Of course I don't believe that. Like my brother, I am an educated man, but I know how dangerous the beliefs of simple people can be."

They had reached the copse, and Frankie inspected a promising tree with a fork in its trunk and a great many sturdy branches. "I've had this lecture already," she said, without looking at her companion. Instead, Frankie was recalling her happy childhood in Seattle, and the big elm that had stood in the backyard. "Don't worry, Alaric. I have no intention of wandering off to the village and getting everyone all worked up again."

With that, Frankie hiked her skirts a little, gripped the trunk of the tree in both hands, and hoisted herself up into the fork.

"Here, now," Alaric protested. "You'll break a limb!"

Frankie proceeded upward, rustling leaves as she went. "Since I know you meant that in only the kindest sense of the word," she called down cheerfully, "I won't take offense." Clinging to the gnarled old tree, she fixed her gaze on the world beyond the orchard, beyond the castle grounds.

The village, made up of tiny daub and wattle structures with thatch roofs, stood in much the same place as it would six hundred years in the future, but the forests to the west looked denser and far more primordial. The remaining three directions were choked with fields, and narrow cow paths served as roads.

Far out, beyond the thriving crops, Frankie saw a
croft or two, but it was plain enough that Braden
was pretty much master of all she surveyed.

"Come down," Alaric wheedled, a thread of irritation vibrating in his voice. "It's not ladylike, climbing
about like that!"

"Surely you've guessed by now that I'm not a
lady," Frankie replied sunnily, settling herself on a
thick branch and smoothing her borrowed skirts. In
doing that, she remembered Braden's sudden mood
change when he'd mentioned having a sister. "Is it
just you and Braden, Alaric, or are there more
Stuart-Ramseys running around the countryside?"

"We have a sister," Alaric answered. "Now get
yourself down here before I'm forced to climb up
after you."

We *have* a sister, he'd said. When Braden had spoken of a female sibling that morning, he'd used the
past tense. "Calm down—I'm an expert tree-climber.
Tell me about your sister. What is her name? Where
does she live?"

Alaric's sigh rose through the maple leaves with a
soft summer breeze. "Her name is Rianne, she's seven-
teen, and Braden sold her off to a distant cousin in
Scotland. Furthermore, he'll have me chained to a wall
and whipped if he finds out I've been talking about
the matter. Now—please come down."

Frankie lingered, swinging her legs and thinking.
"You don't mean he forced her to marry someone
she didn't love?"

"Love." Alaric practically spat the word. "Now,
there's a fatuous notion." He gripped the trunk of
the tree and gave it a slight shake. "Love didn't enter
into the bargain, Francesca. Braden caught Rianne
kissing the chandler's boy, and he was outraged. He

gave her a choice between our esteemed cousin and a long stay in a nunnery and—and I can't imagine why I'm telling you all this."

"Did she choose the cousin over the nunnery, then?"

"No. She said she was going to travel all the way to London and then throw herself into the Thames. *Braden* chose the cousin. He believed Rianne would be better off with a man to keep her out of trouble, and he was probably right."

Frankie was horrified to comprehend just how wide the breach of time and custom between herself and Braden really was. "She should have spit in his eye—he had no right to make such a decree!"

When Alaric replied, which wasn't until several moments of vibrant silence had passed, he sounded confused, nervous, and not a little exasperated. "Braden is a duke. Everyone obeys him, except for the King and the Almighty Himself. Rianne was foolish to anger him in the first place."

Just as Frankie opened her mouth to announce that, in her opinion, the Duke was long overdue for some consciousness raising, a very strange thing happened. A loud thrumming sound filled Frankie's ears, and she felt dizzy, as if she might topple out of the tree. Her vision was blurred and her stomach lurched.

Looking down, she barely made out the figure of Alaric. He was standing eerily still and staring up at her with his mouth open, one hand outspread in a conversational gesture.

Frankie wrapped one arm tightly around the tree trunk and held on. "All right," she said aloud, "what's going on here?"

She heard a rustling sound, saw a glimmer of blue

silk out of the corner of one eye. When she made herself turn her head and look, she was flabbergasted.

Sitting on a branch in the next tree was the wizard she'd seen the day before, peering through the window of the costume shop in Grimsley. He was a tall man, obviously not at home in the high regions of a maple, and he held on to his splendid, pointed hat with one bejeweled hand. His white beard was filled with twigs and parts of leaves, and ice-blue eyes snapped behind round glass spectacles as he glared at Frankie.

"Who are you?" she demanded.

"My name is Merlin, not that it's important," he replied with a distinct lack of enthusiasm. Plainly, he had not situated himself in the branches of a tree, decked out in full wizard gear, to make small talk. "Kindly listen, Miss Whittier, and listen well. We don't have much time."

Frankie swallowed. Merlin, she thought skeptically. Right. She couldn't think why the sudden appearance of a wizard surprised her so much, given all that had gone before, but she was definitely in shock. "Wh-what did you do to him?" she asked, looking down at Alaric, who was still standing down there with his mouth open.

Merlin made a dismissive gesture with one hand and nearly fell out of the tree. "He'll be perfectly all right, more's the pity. It's his job, in fact, to run the Stuart-Ramsey estates into rack and ruin."

Frankie thought of Braden, and how much his small kingdom probably meant to him, and felt wounded. "What about Bra—the Duke? He's the firstborn son. The title and the estates are his."

The wizard sighed. "Not for long," he replied regretfully. "There's a tournament coming up, about a week hence. Sunderlin will be killed, run through with an opponent's blade when sport turns to deadly combat."

"No," Frankie breathed. In that instant, of all instants, she realized that, as incredible as it seemed, she loved Braden. If he died, she might well perish from the grief, no matter how she fought to stay alive. "No, it can't be—I'll warn him!"

"He won't listen."

Frankie was desperate. "Isn't there some way—?"

"Perhaps," Merlin answered grudgingly, and his expression was grim. "I wasn't in favor of your coming here, but since a mistake had been made in the Beginning—"

"A mistake?" Frankie held on tighter to the tree, and her voice came out in a squeak. "What are you talking about? And why *did* I end up here in Merry Olde England?"

"You and Sunderlin were matched, long ago, before the tapestry of time was woven. There was an error, and somehow he was born in the wrong century, to the wrong parents. On some level of your being, you must have known, and come in search of him."

"Impossible," Frankie breathed. It was no comfort that the wizard's remarks rang true, somewhere deep inside her. "I don't know how I made the trip, but I didn't do it on purpose. The whole thing came as a big shock."

"I understand that," Merlin answered, somewhat brusquely. "Well, there's nothing for it. You'll just have to think long and hard of your own time. That should put you back where you belong, though I can't promise you won't find yourself an old woman or a very young child. These matters are not precise, you know. You can only be sure of landing somewhere in your original life span."

Frankie heard the vaguest humming sound, and she sensed that the magician would disappear in a moment, and that Alaric was already beginning to stir from his enchantment. "Never mind all that," she blurted. "Just tell me how to help Braden!"

For the first time Merlin smiled, but the expression in his eyes was regretful. "Love is the answer to every question," he said, and then, between one instant and the next, he was gone. He didn't even take the time to do a fade-out.

Frankie hesitated a few moments, collecting herself, then shinnied quickly down the tree, practically landing on a befuddled Alaric, who had just started to climb up after her. Gaining the ground, she lifted her skirts, without pausing to offer even a word of explanation, and ran toward the castle as if all eternity hinged on haste.

Four

FRANKIE found Braden on the other side of the castle, his upper body protected by chain mail, wielding his fancy sword. His opponent was a young knight, obviously eager to prove his prowess on the field of battle.

Thinking only of what Merlin, the magician, had just told her—that Braden would die by the sword in a week's time—Frankie hesitated just briefly. She would have marched right into the center of the large circle of loose dirt if Alaric hadn't crooked an arm around her waist and stopped her.

The small fracas drew Braden's attention, and in that brief moment of distraction, his adversary struck, reckless in his enthusiasm. Bringing his sword downward, from shoulder height, he made a deep gash in the Duke's right thigh.

There were eight or ten men crowded around, watching the morning exercise, and a shout of outrage went up as blood stained Braden's gray leggings to crimson.

For Frankie, all of this took place in a pounding haze, rather like a slow-motion sequence in a movie. In reality, of course, it happened in the space of seconds. She screamed and struggled so violently that Alaric could not hold her.

Braden was still standing when she fought her way through the crowd of men pressed close around him, but she was alarmed by the ghastly paleness of his face. He looked at her as though she were an enemy, as though she herself had wounded him.

There were mutterings in the small assembly, and Frankie heard the word *witch*, but she didn't think of the implications. All that mattered then was Braden, that he be well and whole, and somehow saved from the fate that awaited him.

A rotund bearded man in coarse robes took charge. "Steady him," he ordered, crouching at Braden's feet. Two men immediately came forward to stand close, lest their leader need them. The big man tied a band of cloth around the Duke's upper thigh, just above the deep cut, and pulled it tight.

Braden flinched and swayed slightly, but remained on his feet. His gaze, accusatory and bewildered, had never left Frankie's face. "Continue with your practice," he said to his men, and then he limped toward her.

Only when Braden was standing close did Frankie realize that her cheeks were wet with tears.

"I'm sorry," she said brokenly. "I didn't mean—"

"Come along, Your Lordship," the heavy man interceded. "You'll be in need of some looking after."

Braden raised one hand and, with the rough side of his thumb, wiped Frankie's cheek. Then one corner of his mouth rose in the merest hint of a smile. "What was so important, Francesca, that you would burst into the middle of swordplay like that?"

Frankie shouldered aside the man who'd been hovering close to Braden and slipped under the Duke's arm to help support him. She couldn't very well explain about Merlin, not with so many superstitious ears about. Besides, she was more concerned, for the moment, with the state of Braden's health. Her thoughts had shifted to medieval medical practices.

"Never mind," she said, feeling injured because Braden was. "We can discuss that later. You're not going to let these yokels put leeches on you, I hope— you've lost enough blood as it is, and the possibility of infection—"

The heavy man, who was supporting Braden on the other side, leaned around the Duke's chest to glower at Frankie. "Yokels?"

An exasperated sigh burst from Braden's lips. "Perhaps you two could argue this out later, when I may be spared the pleasure of listening."

Alaric, who had been following the small party, sprinted ahead to walk backward in front of Braden, talking a mile a minute. "I tried to stop her," he said, taking care not to meet Frankie's gaze. "God's knees, Braden, but you look like a walking corpse—"

Frankie tuned him out, concentrating instead on the Duke's needs. She was no doctor, of course, but she'd had intensive instruction in first aid while being trained as a flight attendant. She wasn't about to leave Braden to the mercies of people who might pack his wound with sheep dung or drain away still more of his blood.

They entered the Great Hall, and the smoky atmosphere made Frankie's eyes burn. Braden stumbled once as they moved toward the stairs, and then his knees buckled.

"No farther," ordered the heavy man, who had taken charge from the first. "You must lie down, milord."

"You make much of little, Gilford," Braden said, and Frankie heard affection in his voice, as well as impatience and no small amount of pain.

Nevertheless, one of the great trestle tables lining the Hall was cleared of salt cellars and wine ewers, and Braden lay down on the surface without further protest.

Gilford looked across the table at Frankie, who stood staunchly on the other side, keeping her stubborn vigil. "You are in the way, wench. Leave us."

"Not on your life," Frankie replied.

Braden chuckled, but he was looking worse with every passing moment, even though the tourniquet had slowed the bleeding from his thigh. "Don't waste your breath arguing with her," he warned his friend. "Francesca's opinions are as immovable as the walls of this castle."

Gilford treated her to a scathing glare. "Then perhaps she can make herself useful in other ways. By fetching wine, and my herbal kit."

Frankie tightened her grip on Braden's hand. "Alaric can do those things, or one of the servants. I'm staying right here."

Alaric needed no urging; he rushed off to get the things Gilford wanted. In the meantime, the castle medicine man took a knife from the folds of his robe and began cutting away Braden's bloody leggings.

Frankie swayed slightly when she saw just how bad the wound was, but she willed new strength into her knees and somehow stilled the tempest in her stomach. "Shouldn't someone be boiling water?" she asked shakily.

"The water is filthy," Gilford said. "I will clean the area with wine."

His statement jarred Frankie, and she lifted her gaze to his face again. "You know about antisepsis?" she asked.

"You," Gilford replied, "are not the only stranger in these here parts, young woman."

Frankie's mouth fell open. Automatically she stroked Braden's sweat-dampened forehead with one hand, but it was the castle physician who held her attention. "When?" she asked in barely a whisper. There was no one else close by, since Alaric had gone off on his errand and the sword practice had continued outside, per Braden's orders.

"Seventy-two," Gilford said. "I came here to get away from my practice in London for a while—I was suffering from what you Americans call burnout. Went to sleep there, woke up here. For a long time I thought I'd lost my mind."

Frankie nodded her understanding, but could say nothing. Merlin hadn't mentioned that there were other time-travelers abroad, but then, they hadn't talked for very long.

"What in the name of God's Great Aunt are you two talking about?" Braden asked, slurring his words. He was waxen, and although his flesh felt cold, he was sweating.

"Cabbages and kings," Gilford told the Duke. "Just lie there, please, and conserve your strength." Alaric returned with the wine and the doctor's herbal kit, and Gilford used the alcohol to clean the wound. Braden drifted in and out of consciousness, and the physician talked to Frankie in even tones as he worked. "I've never wanted to go back, you know. Strange as it seems, I feel I belong here. What about you? What part of the Rebel Colonies do you hail from?"

Frankie was trying to funnel her own strength into Braden, and she didn't look up from his face when she answered. "It was nineteen-ninety-three when I left," she said. "And I'm from Seattle, in Washington State."

"Hmmmm," said Gilford, packing Braden's wound with an herbal concoction. "He's going to have a nasty scar, here, but I've no catgut to stitch him up with. I was in Seattle once, on a holiday tour. My wife and I flew there by way of New York and Chicago and took a sailing ship up the coast to Alaska. Spectacular experience."

Braden laughed stupidly. "Flying," he said. "There's a picture, Gilford—you, flying. Didn't your arms get tired?"

Despite the fact that her eyes were red and puffy from crying, Frankie laughed, too. "Do you miss your life in the twentieth century?" she asked Gilford when she'd had a few moments to regain her composure. "Your wife must be very worried."

Gilford sighed. "I suppose I'm on some police roster," he said. "One of those pesky people who've just disappeared from the face of the earth without leaving a trace behind. As for my wife's state of mind, well, Zenobia is the resilient type. By now, she's probably sold my practice and remarried."

"You've been here a long time, then?"

"Roughly twenty years, now," Gilford answered, binding Braden's thigh with clean cloth taken from his own supply kit. "I've been happy the whole while, too."

Frankie studied the doctor closely. "How did you know I was a time-traveler like you?"

At last Gilford favored her with a smile. A rather nice one, as a matter of fact. "I'm a doctor. After only one look at you, I knew you'd grown up in a world where there was relatively clean water to drink, healthy nutrition, excellent medical care, and the like. Most of the people around us, in case you haven't noticed, are rather fragile creatures."

Frankie still held Braden's hand, and unconsciously she cradled it between her breasts. "What of the Duke? He's certainly nothing like them."

Gilford smiled at Braden, who had drifted off to sleep. No doubt the herbs the doctor had administered were responsible for that. "No, he isn't. He's a misfit, like you and me."

Frankie liked Gilford, despite their getting off on the wrong foot earlier, and it was a great comfort to know she was not the only one who'd ever found herself in the wrong century. "Are there others?" she asked.

"Other time-travelers?" Gilford was using the last of the wine to wash Braden's blood from his hands. "Almost certainly. If it happened to us, then surely someone else has experienced the same phenomenon. You, however, are the first such sojourner I've had the good fortune to meet." He summoned Alaric, who had been hovering at a little distance throughout the procedure, and sent him off for men to carry Braden upstairs. "You've been very careless so far, Francesca," the medical man scolded after Alaric hurried away on his mission. "These people fear what they do not understand, and what they fear, they destroy. You must guard your tongue, in the future, and try not to be so brazen."

Frankie felt faint and gripped the edge of the table to steady herself. "I'm no fool, Doctor—I don't want to be hanged, or burned at the stake, and I promise I'll be more careful. At the moment, though, it's Braden I'm worried about—is he going to make it? How long will he be laid up with this injury?" She held her breath while she waited for Gilford's answer.

The portly time-traveler sighed again and folded his bulky arms. "Sunderlin will recover, I'm sure— he has the personal tenacity and physical strength of a mountain goat. And my guess is, he'll be up and walking about on that leg within a day or two, though I'd much prefer that he rest."

Frankie was torn, feeling both joy and terrible desolation. Braden would get well, that was wonderful. But if he truly was back on his feet in a matter of days, he would still participate in the tournament in a week's time. And that meant he would die.

"You're his doctor! Can't you order him to stay in bed until he's had a chance to mend?"

Sadly Gilford shook his head. "No one keeps this man from doing exactly as he wishes," he said.

Frankie confided in him about her encounter with Merlin that day, and told of the dire prediction the magician had made, but only in the barest detail. She felt drained; so much had happened, just since she'd opened her eyes that morning, that it seemed she'd lived a whole decade without taking a breath.

Alaric returned with two big men, and they carried Braden to his room. Frankie sat with Braden until midafternoon, then, satisfied that he was sleeping comfortably, went off to get some fresh air and some perspective on the situation.

She was drawn to the chapel, which she found by trial and error on the ground floor of the castle, well away from the Great Hall and the usually busy kitchen. She was not a particularly religious person, but a spiritual one, and sitting in that small chamber, with its rough-hewn benches, rows of unlit candles, and towering wooden cross, was like nestling in the soul of God.

"Show me what to do," she whispered, clasping her hands together tightly in her lap. "Please. Show me how to save Braden from the sword."

No ready answer came to Frankie, and yet she was restored by the mystical peace of the place. It seemed then that there was indeed a solution, and that she would find it.

After an hour she went back to Braden's chamber and found him sitting up in bed, drinking ale from a wooden mug. His color was better, but his mood was sour indeed.

"Why, Francesca?" he demanded hoarsely, virtually impaling her with his sharp gaze. "Why did you interfere with the fighting that way? The distraction could have gotten me killed."

Frankie kept her distance, even though she knew instinctively that Braden would never hurt her. "I told you I was sorry. And I was coming to—to warn you about something."

Braden's brows knitted together for a moment as he frowned. "Warn me? About what?"

She swallowed. This was not going to be easy. Braden probably wouldn't believe her story, and she didn't blame him. "I met a wizard today—his name was Merlin. He said you were going to be killed a week from now, fighting in a tournament."

Braden refilled his cup from a jug on the table next to his bed and took an audible gulp, then filled his mouth again, so that his cheeks bulged. He swallowed once more, and his voice came out sounding raspy when he spoke. "A wizard," he repeated with irony.

Frankie's temper flared when she heard the quiet annoyance and thinly veiled pity in his tone. "Yes."

The Duke was not looking at her when he spoke again. "Alaric was with you. Did he see this man of magic, too?"

Braden's manner told Frankie it was Alaric's presence he was concerned about, not the wizard's. Despite her frustration, and her fear, she felt a little thrill of pleasure at the realization that Braden was jealous.

"No," she answered, gaining confidence. "Alaric didn't see anything. He was frozen, between one heartbeat and the next, and freed only when Merlin permitted it."

Braden reached out suddenly, grasped her hand, and squeezed. His face was filled with an anguish Frankie suspected was unrelated to the wound in his thigh. "Francesca," he whispered, "promise me, please, that you will not speak thus, of wizards and the like, to anyone but me."

She sat down on the edge of his bed and smiled softly. In those moments Frankie was filled with immeasurable joy and equally unfathomable sorrow, for it was then that she grasped the terrible, wonderful miracle that had occurred. She was in love with Sunderlin, and that love was an eternal thing, meant to outlive both of them.

She smoothed Sunderlin's rumpled, dusty hair back from his forehead. "I do promise to try, Braden," she said gently. "But I'm impulsive, and sometimes words are out of my mouth before I know I was even thinking them."

Braden lifted her hand to his lips, sent a charge of emotion through her merely by kissing her knuckles. "You and Gilford were saying very strange things today," he recalled after some moments had passed. "He has always refused to explain his odd talents and beliefs. Will you refuse as well?"

Careful not to bump Braden's injured leg, Frankie made a place for herself beside him, resting her back against his shoulder, turning her face into his neck. "I'll tell you everything," she said. "But I'm so afraid, Braden. So very afraid."

"Why?" He entangled a finger in one of her curls, twisted with an idle gentleness that somehow stirred her heart. "I know there's something different about you, but I'll not declare you angel *or* witch, and I promise I'll protect you from the whole of the world if need be."

Frankie was touched to the core of her spirit. Why, she wondered sadly, couldn't she have met this man in her own time, where they might have had a happy life together? Here, they had a mere week to share.

She sighed, settled closer to Braden, and began to talk. She told him about Seattle, and other modern cities. She described flying to New York in a jumbo jet, and then crossing the Atlantic the same way, to land in London. Braden listened to the whole story, in what was probably a stunned silence, never interrupting.

Frankie spoke of her trip to the village of Grimsley, the Medieval Fair that was held there every year, for the tourists, her attempt to rent a costume, the glimpse she'd caught of Merlin through the shop window, her unscheduled trip through time.

When it was over, Braden shifted both himself and Frankie, so that he could look deep into her eyes. "How could one person devise such a tale?"

Tears brimmed along her lower lashes. "I'm not making anything up, Braden," she said. "It's all true. And I saw that same wizard again this morning, like I told you. He said you were supposed to be born in my time, the future, but there was some sort of mistake and you ended up here. And you're going to be killed in a tournament next week, unless you call it off."

His face hardened, and Frankie saw in his light brown eyes both bewilderment and the desire to trust her. "I cannot do such a thing. I am not a coward, and I won't have the whole of England saying I heeded the words of a witch!"

Frankie wriggled off the bed and stood, disappointed and stung even though she'd known he wouldn't readily believe her story. "All right. You're a hardheaded, arrogant, opinionated *male*, and as such you aren't about to listen to reason. Well, that's just fine, but I don't intend to hang around here, caring more with every day that passes, only to see you run through with a sword!"

She would have turned and fled the room then, and maybe the castle and the village, too, but Braden caught hold of her hand and held it fast.

" 'Caring more with every day that passes,' is it?" he asked in a low, teasing voice. "Confess, witch—are you falling in love with me?"

It was worse, Frankie admitted to herself. She'd already fallen. But that didn't mean she had to let

Braden know. "Of course not." She thought fast. "Alaric is more my type."

"What?" Braden snapped the word, and his color, so good a moment before, had gone waxen again.

Frankie looked away, biting her lip. She couldn't say any more; the lie was too profound, the truth too holy.

"Look at me, Francesca," Braden ordered gravely.

She looked, not because of his command, but because she was hungry for the sight of him. And she despised that hunger, even as she succumbed to it.

"Whatever you are, witch or angel," Braden said, "you've managed to cast an enchantment over me. I must have you, no matter what else I gain or lose. In you I will plant my children, and all my hopes of joy and passion."

Frankie stared at him, dumbfounded, wondering at the new universe that had sprung to life inside her, a vast expanse of love for this one man.

He smiled and caressed her cheek, then pushed her off the bed, where she scrambled to get and keep her footing.

"Summon Mordag," he said, gesturing toward the bellpull. "I would have him fetch a priest."

Five

FRANKIE recovered some of her aplomb only after she'd given the bellrope a good yank. "Braden, stop and think. We can't be married—we're from different universes! Besides, you don't even know me, really, and I don't know you, either."

"Happens all the time," Braden said, settling back on the pillows and folding his great arms. "My mother came from the North to be wed to my father—the first time they laid eyes on each other was at the ceremony." He hoisted himself from the bed, and Frankie winced as he flexed his injured leg. "That marriage went well enough."

Frankie ignored the comment. "Shouldn't you be lying down?"

Braden was walking back and forth over the rushes, his jaw set, his face colorless as he dealt with the inevitable pain. He did not reply, except to pinion her with a brief, fierce glare.

Mordag appeared soon enough, bowing and scraping and plainly alarmed that his master was up and about so soon after sustaining a wound. He chattered away in Old English and distractedly Frankie wondered why she could understand Braden and Alaric, but not the ordinary people.

Braden told Mordag to go into the village and bring back the priest, but before that, he was to send up women servants to groom "the lady" for a wedding.

"I haven't agreed to your proposal yet, you know," Frankie pointed out, somewhat shakily. "You're being a bit hasty, don't you think?"

"No," Sunderlin answered succinctly. His color was returning now, and he moved more easily. "Even now my son and heir may already nestle in your womb. There will be no question of his legitimacy."

"It's equally possible that there is no child," Frankie reasoned. "We've only—we've only been together once, you know."

Sunderlin smiled. "Once is often enough. I'm sure that's true even in your faraway world."

Frankie gaped at him for a moment, then blurted out, "You believe me, then?"

He came to her, fondly lifted a tendril of her chin-length hair, rubbed it between his fingers, and let it fall back into place. "At first," he reflected with a bemused grin, "I thought you had been shorn in some asylum while suffering from a brain fever. But reason tells me that you are too sound, not only of body but of disposition, to have been through such

an illness." Braden paused, sighed, kissed her forehead. "Yes, I think I believe you, Francesca, though
I don't claim to understand how such a thing could
happen."

Frankie laid her head against Braden's chest, felt
his hands come to rest lightly on her shoulder blades.
She was almost as confused by the suddenness and
depth of her feelings for Sunderlin as she was by the
knowledge that she had indeed traveled through
time.

"Take me to London," she said in a desperate
bid to spirit Braden away from Sunderlin Keep and
the tournament.

"Please, darling—as soon as we're married."

Braden curved a finger under her chin, lifted her
head so that he could look directly into her face. "I
will be happy to take you to London, there to pres-
ent you at court. *After* the tournament."

An overwhelming grief surged up inside Frankie,
and she marveled because at the same time she felt
a powerful, greedy joy. "Do you wish to die?" she
demanded angrily, leaning back in his arms but not
quite able to leave his embrace. "Why else would
you ignore such a warning?"

He sighed, and she saw the pain of his physical
injury flicker in his eyes. "I cannot run away from
what has been given me to do," he said with gentle
reason. "It is a matter of honor. Besides, if my death
has been ordained by the powers of heaven as it
would seem, it will do no good for me to flee to
London."

Before Frankie could offer further argument—and
even then she knew it would be fruitless to try anyway—several female servants came to collect her.
She was taken to a smaller chamber down the hall,

where a large copper tub had been set before the fire.

Frankie had a bath, her hair was washed and brushed, and then the women dressed her in a slightly musty-smelling but nonetheless beautiful white velvet gown. She went back to the master chamber to fetch the wreath of dried flowers she'd brought with her from the other time, and there was no sign of Braden.

He awaited her in the chapel, pale and grim, and yet with a fire burning in his caramel eyes as he watched her come toward him. He had to be in serious pain, but he'd learned to transcend it, probably through his training as a knight.

What are you doing, Francesca Whittier? Frankie's good sense demanded, even as she hurried up the narrow aisle to stand beside her future husband. This man isn't real—he's a ghost, a pile of moldering dust lying in some crypt!

Frankie shook her head slightly and sent the ghoulish thoughts scattering. Braden was a miracle, and he might well be taken from her all too soon, either by the sword or by her own unexpected return to the modern world. She would live breath by breath and heartbeat by heartbeat, cherishing every moment she was given to spend with Braden.

The priest was a friar, straight out of a storybook, and Frankie didn't understand a word he said. She simply mumbled and gave a slight nod whenever he turned an expectant look on her. All too soon the romantic, strangely magical ceremony was over, and Braden bent his head to place a light kiss on Frankie's mouth.

She lifted her eyes to meet his, inwardly stunned at the power and breadth of her love for him. It was

as if it had always existed within her, a vast plain of
the spirit, infinite and rich, only now discovered.

Tears brimmed along her lashes; she gave a little
cry of mingled sorrow and joy, and threw her arms
around his neck. This caused a twittering among the
few guests, but Frankie didn't care. Every second
was a pearl of great price; not one would be wasted.

Braden smiled, shook his head, as if marveling at
something too amazing to mention aloud, and tugged
gently at one of the ribbons trailing from her crown
of flowers.

Frankie had expected that she and her groom
would return to the bridal chamber straightaway, and
she was unabashedly ready. Instead, however, a celebration of sorts was to be held in the Great Hall;
musicians and mummers and jesters had been com-
mandeered from the village fair, and there were
mountains of food.

Despite the festive air of the place, Frankie had
no illusions that the people of Braden's world ac-
cepted her as their mistress. She saw in more than
one pair of eyes that she was still feared, still
suspected.

While Braden held court at the head table, en-
joying the toasts and guarded congratulations of his
men-at-arms, Gilford approached Frankie and took
her elbow lightly in one hand.

"Come with me," he whispered urgently. "Now."

Frankie didn't want to stray too far from Braden's
side, but she was alarmed by the doctor's earnest-
ness. They slipped into a small courtyard, tucked
away behind the Great Hall, where bees bumbled
and buzzed among blowsy red and yellow roses.

"If you know a way to get back to the twentieth
century," Gilford whispered after making certain

they were alone, "you'd best be about it. There's talk among the servants and the others that you've bewitched the Duke somehow—they're blaming you for his wound, and they say no power less than the devil's own could have made him marry you." The doctor took both her hands in his own and squeezed. "Please—do not tarry in this place. If you can't will yourself home somehow, then we must smuggle you out of the keep and hide you somewhere."

She opened her mouth to protest, but Gilford never gave her a chance.

"Frankie," he said, "these people are terrified of you. They want to burn you as a witch."

"Braden would never allow it!" Frankie said, but she was cold with fear there in that warm, fragrant garden.

"Sunderlin may not be around after the tournament, if your wizard is to be believed. I beg of you, Frankie, save yourself both heartache and a truly terrible death if you can."

She pulled her hands free of his and hugged herself, but that did not still the trembling. "Merlin did say something about thinking long and hard of my own time, as if that would make me go back. He also said I could end up at any stage of my life—"

"Do it, then."

Frankie shook her head. "No," she said. "I'm here now, and there must be some reason for that. I'm going to see it through."

Gilford sighed heavily and gestured toward the west. "At least let me take you to the nunnery, just beyond the fells, where you'll be safe. I can enter and leave the keep whenever I wish, and you could hide in my cart, under some straw or blankets."

For a moment Frankie considered the idea. In the

end, however, she discarded it because it meant being parted from Braden, even by a short distance.

"I'm staying," she said, starting around Gilford to return to the celebration. After all, she was the bride, and her handsome groom awaited.

Gilford caught her arm. "That is a very foolish decision," he bit out. His fingers cut into the tender flesh on the inside of her elbow. "I beg you to reconsider."

Frankie looked down at her white velvet dress, and when she raised her eyes again, her vision was blurred with tears. "I must get back to my husband," she said softly. Then, reluctantly, Gilford freed her, and she hurried back into the Great Hall.

Strong as he was, Braden had had an especially hard day. After only a few boisterous toasts, each followed by a tankard of ale, he began to yawn. It was a relief to Frankie, who had been feeling more alienated from the guests with every passing moment, when he signaled that it was time for them to leave the festivities.

Once they were in their chamber, and the ever-present Mordag had been sent away, Frankie gave her bridegroom an unceremonious push toward the bed. Her reason was anything but romantic. "You need to rest," she scolded "You're dead on your feet."

Braden limped to the bedside, sat down gingerly on its edge, then stretched out with a low groan of mingled relief and suffering. "Now, there's a memorable saying. I suppose someone is going to write that one down someday, as well as the remark about the serpent's tooth."

Frankie smiled and bent over her husband to kiss his forehead. He looked very handsome in his clean blue leggings and purple silk tunic, even though the bandages on his thigh made for an unsightly bulge.

"Someday," she agreed. "I love you, Braden. Whatever happens to us, please remember that."

The groom reached up, touched the side of the bride's nose with a fingertip, then yawned again. "I'll just rest a while now, Duchess, then we'll enjoy the traditional consummation."

Frankie laughed, though she felt as much like crying. "What a poet you are, Braden Stuart-Ramsey, Duke of Sunderlin."

He grinned, though his eyes were closed, and only moments later he was snoring.

Frankie sat beside him for a time, trying to assimilate his presence somehow, as if it were medicine to her soul, and then went out onto the crude stone terrace. There, she had a view of the village, and the stream flowing through it like a wide ribbon of shining foil in the sunshine.

Standing high above the moat, which was filled with stinking, stagnate water, Frankie again considered her plight. Never before had she had a keener sense of what was meant by the phrase, *living for the moment.* She had nothing else—no past and, perhaps, no future. Just this precious wrinkle in time, where she and Braden were tucked away together.

When Braden stirred, after an hour or so, Frankie went back inside the chamber, removed her improvised wedding dress and the wreath of dried flowers, and lay down with her husband. Slowly, and with great reverence, the Duke introduced his Duchess to pleasures even sweeter and more fiery than those she had known before.

It was the next morning, when Braden had gone back to oversee the sword practice despite his wounded leg, that Frankie saw the wizard again. She was sitting in the hidden garden, the one off the Great Hall that Gilford had taken her to the day before, when she suddenly looked up and found Merlin standing in front of her.

On a man of less commanding presence, the magician's robes and pointed hat might have looked silly, but he carried them off with a flourish.

"So you've married the Duke," he said, arms folded. "That was very foolish, indeed."

Frankie's heart had shinnied up her rib cage and made the leap to her throat, she'd been so startled by the magician's sudden materialization in the garden. Now the organ sank back to its normal place— or perhaps a little lower. At the same time she lifted her chin in a gesture of polite defiance.

"I love Braden."

"Perhaps," Merlin conceded, "but as I told you before, this is not meant to be. An error was made at the Beginning, yes, but what is done is done. Sunderlin shall perish, ere the week is out, and you must go back where you belong before you are executed for sorcery."

"By thinking long and hard of home?" Frankie sounded sarcastic, she knew, but she couldn't help it. She was terrified and confused, and those elements combined to make her tongue sharp. "What is this, the Land of Oz? Shouldn't I just click my heels together and say—"

"Enough," Merlin broke in, exasperated. "Time is a creation of the mind. Your other life is not at the end of the universe; indeed, it is so close you could reach out and touch it. Think of your own world, Francesca. Think of it!"

His words enchanted her somehow; she recalled

Seattle, with its hills, its busy harbor, its bustle and energy. For the merest fraction of a moment, she saw flashes of old brick around her, heard the horns of taxicabs as they bumped over the streets in Pioneer Square. For one tiny portion of a single heartbeat, she was back there, standing on the corner of Yesler Way and First Avenue South, only a stone's throw from her shop. A little more concentration, just a little, and she would truly have been there, as solid and real as the old brick building she knew so well.

Still, Frankie's heart was with Braden, and she followed it back in a single cosmic leap. She was perspiring, cold and sick, as she sat clutching the edge of the ancient stone bench in the garden of old roses, struggling to stay long after the need had passed.

"Fool," Merlin said, but in a kind tone. Then, as quickly as he'd appeared, he vanished into the soft, misty air of the morning.

Frankie braved the kitchen after that, there purloining a basketful of various foods from beneath the cook's disapproving nose, and ventured cautiously to the practice grounds. This time, heaven be thanked, she did not surprise Braden into being stabbed. In fact, he was on the sidelines, calling out instructions to other combatants, and when he sensed Frankie's presence, he tossed a smile in her direction and then came hobbling after it.

Even with a limp, she thought, he was a magnificent man. She pictured him in jeans and a half-shirt as he moved toward her, then in a perfectly tailored three-piece suit. Both prospects were delicious.

"I've brought the stuff for a picnic," she said. "We can sit under those maple trees on the far side of the grounds."

Frankie had half expected Braden to refuse her invitation, but instead he took the basket from her and started toward the place she'd chosen for their picnic.

An idea was forming in her mind, and as they ate, she told Braden more about modern-day Seattle. While keeping herself as detached as possible, lest she be snatched back, she tried to make her husband see the buses and cars, the paved roadways, the concrete and steel buildings that loomed against the sky. Her theory was that, if he could imagine the place, perhaps he could also go there somehow, with her. After all, Merlin had once said that Braden truly belonged in that other world, and not in the much cruder and more dangerous one around them.

They lay side by side in the grass for a time, once they'd eaten, and Braden plucked a dandelion from the grass and tickled Frankie's chin with its ghostly down. "I wish I could make love to you right here," he said hoarsely. "We are, of course, being watched."

"Of course," Frankie agreed sadly, catching his hand in hers, squeezing tightly. "Oh, Braden, won't you please call off the tournament? For me?"

He raised her knuckles to his mouth, brushed his lips across them in a caress as light as the passage of a butterfly. "I'm sorry, Francesca. I would do almost anything for you, but I cannot abandon my honor as a man."

Frankie was suddenly flushed with conviction, frustration, and fear. "Your *honor*? Good Lord, Braden, what is honorable about suicide? That's what this is, you know, because you've been warned and you still insist on fighting!"

He smoothed her wind-tousled hair back from her

face. "I can do nothing else, beloved—this is who I am. Besides, I am among the best swordsmen in England."

She closed her eyes tightly, seeking some inner balance, and then nodded. There was no use in arguing; that was clear. Braden was as set on following his path as she was on following her own.

They finished their meal of cold venison, dried fruit, and even drier bread, and then Braden insisted on going back to the field of practice. While Frankie could certainly see the sense in his desire to be as expert a swordsman as possible, she wished there were no need for fighting.

It was a brutal time in history, she thought as they walked back together, her hand tucked into his. And yet, Frankie had to admit, her own era was fraught with peril, too. Each had its pestilences, its widespread poverty, its violence and prejudice. The differences were really pretty superficial.

Now that she'd had a chance to compare the two, however, Frankie knew with a certainty that she preferred her own niche, far away in the tempestuous nineteen-nineties. The only hitch was that she would have to leave Braden to get back there.

Frankie stopped, shading her eyes from the sun and watching as her husband moved haltingly, and yet with that profound confidence of his, toward the field of practice. He must have felt Frankie's gaze, for, although he did not look back, he raised one hand in a gesture she knew was meant for her.

Inside the keep Frankie made her way through cool, shadowy passageways until she reached the chapel. There she sat alone on the bench closest to the wooden cross beside the altar, her hands folded. The next few days passed in much the same manner as that one had. Braden practiced incessantly, refusing to rest, and Frankie prepared a picnic meal for their noon repast. In the afternoons she sat in the quiet sanctuary of the chapel, offering wordless petitions, prayers of presence rather than pleading.

The nights, ah, the nights. Those were the most delicious, the most bittersweet, the most glorious and tragic times of all.

Braden and Frankie loved until they were gasping and exhausted, until their bodies rebelled and tumbled into the dark, bottomless well of sleep. Always, when the morning came, they loved again.

Day by day, knights and nobles from other parts of the country arrived, with pageantry and fanfare, some housed within the keep, others pitching brightly colored tents outside the walls. The summer fair would soon culminate in a tournament that, according to Gilford, had been a local tradition since the time of William the Conqueror. It was even rumored that the king himself, His Royal Majesty, Edward III, might put in an appearance.

Frankie cared about none of this. When she awakened to the sound of trumpets that morning just a week after her arrival, she knew her own personal Judgment Day had arrived.

Six

THE maidservants murmured among themselves as they attended Frankie that morning of the tournament. She was decked out in a lovely gown of rose-colored silk, trimmed at cuff and hem with fine lace. Her hair was brushed and then pulled into a French braid, with ribbon to match the dress woven in for ornamentation.

Frankie was not seeing her reflection in the looking glass affixed to the wall behind the dressing table. The sounds of the trumpets echoed in her ears, and her heart was pounding with a steadily rising fear.

This day, unless she found some way to prevent it, the man she loved more than her own soul would die. He would no longer exist, either in this world or the one she knew, and she found the thought unbearable.

It was a word snagged from the conversation of

the sulky maids attending her that caught Frankie's attention.

"—witch—"

She rose from the bench where she'd sat and turned on the two women. Both lowered their eyes.

"What are you saying about me?" she demanded.

The reply came not from the servants, but from Alaric, who had entered the chamber unannounced and was now helping himself to a piece of fruit from a clay bowl on a table just inside the door.

"They're certain you're the devil's mistress," he said idly, his hand hovering over one piece of fruit and then another. Finally he settled on a speckled pear. "God be thanked for the Italians and their sunny orchards." Despite his cheerful manner, he spoke sternly to the maids, and they vanished, but not before casting looks of mingled terror and resentment in Frankie's direction.

Frankie was only slightly more comfortable in Alaric's presence. He, after all, was slated by the fates to take over the estates following Braden's death and destroy everything the family had built over the centuries.

"Braden isn't here," she said, keeping the breadth of Sunderlin's writing desk between them.

Alaric ran his dark gaze over her, then sighed. "What a lovely, lovely thing you are, Francesca. My brother is a fortunate man."

Frankie said nothing; she knew Alaric had not come to praise Braden. Perhaps he'd even known all along that his elder brother was already out greeting visiting nobles and their knights.

After taking a bite from the pear and wiping the juice from his mouth and chin with a forearm, Alaric set the core aside and regarded Frankie in silence for a time. Then, hands resting on his hips, he said solicitously, "Poor Francesca. This, I fear, will not be a good day for either you or my dear brother."

She clutched the table's edge, felt herself go pale, and yet kept her chin high and her eyes fiery with rebellion. "Why do you say that, Alaric?" she dared to ask. "Are you plotting against Braden, and thus against me?"

Alaric chuckled. "There is no plot," he said. "But I sense danger, the way one sometimes senses the approach of a storm in otherwise perfect weather. I have a cart ready and waiting at the south gate, Francesca. It's not too late to escape."

"And leave my husband? Never."

"How is it that you've become so attached to him in such a short time?" Alaric inquired with what sounded like genuine puzzlement. He shrugged when she didn't reply, and went on. "True, Braden is much-praised as a lover. But he is not the only man in the world who knows how to give a woman pleasure."

Frankie felt her cheeks turn crimson. As far as she was concerned, Braden *was* the only man in the world, period, for she wanted no other. And she wasn't about to discuss something so personal as her husband's sexual prowess with Alaric or anyone else. "I love him," she said honestly and with a certain quiet ferocity. "Now, please leave me. It's time I joined my husband."

Alaric did not leave; instead, he crooked one arm. "I know, milady," he answered. "I have been sent to escort you. The Duke is busy welcoming his guests, you see, and as a younger son, I am expected to serve as his emissary."

Frankie glared at her brother-in-law for a moment,

keeping her distance. "There must be no more talk of my sneaking away in a cart," she warned. "No matter what happens, I will not leave Braden's side."

"Rash words," Alaric replied, not unkindly. "I hope you do not come to regret them."

With the greatest reluctance Frankie took Alaric's arm and allowed him to squire her out of the bedroom, along the wide passageway, and down the enormous staircase to the Great Hall. There, an enormous crowd had gathered, the women chattering, the children running in every direction, the men laughing together and hoisting pints of ale.

At Frankie's appearance, however, a buzz moved through the group, and then there was utter silence. It took all her courage not to cower against Alaric's side when every person raised their eyes to stare.

Alaric called out something to the people, and Frankie knew he was presenting her as the new mistress of Sunderlin Keep even though she didn't comprehend the actual words. The room seemed to quiver for a moment, with that special kind of silence that indicates strong emotion. Then, here and there, a tradesman or a knight or a squire dropped to one knee and lowered his head in deference to the Duke's bride.

The women eyed her narrowly, far more suspicious than the men, but some of them executed grudging curtsies as she passed with Alaric.

It was something of a relief when they passed beneath the high archway and onto the castle grounds.

Colorful tents dotted the landscape, inside the walls as well as out, and one could not turn around without seeing a juggler or a pie merchant or a musician or a nobleman in grand clothes. Frankie took in the spectacle—that could not be helped—but she was too nervous to really appreciate what she was seeing and hearing.

Where was Braden?

Alaric took her to the field of practice, where a long, fencelike structure had been set up, along with a grandstand of sorts and still more tents. Keeping Frankie close to his side with a certain subtle force, Alaric explained that the wooden wall was called a tilt, and that it was designed to keep the horses from colliding during the joust.

Frankie was shading her eyes from the morning sun and searching the crowd for Braden. She thirsted for the sight of him, yearned for the sound of his voice.

But Alaric did not seem anxious to find his brother. He gestured toward the drawbridge, which lay open across the moat. It was packed with travelers coming in and out, on foot, in carts, and on horseback.

"It would be easy to pass through unnoticed, milady," he said. "We have only to exchange those rich silks of yours for a peasant's rags and muss up your lovely hair a bit—"

Just then Frankie spotted Braden. He was standing in a circle of men, smiling, and as she watched, he threw back his magnificent head in a burst of happy laughter. The sound struck Frankie's spirit like one of the spiked steel balls she'd seen in the chamber where weapons were kept.

She pulled free of Alaric, despite his attempt to hold her, and set off toward her husband. It was probably a breach of some masculine code for her to stride right up to him that way, but Frankie was past caring about such things, if she ever had. Her only plan—and a pitifully thin plan it was, too—was to hover close to Braden throughout the day and somehow protect him.

On some level Frankie knew this would probably turn out to be an impossible feat, but she had no other choice but to try. She could not simply abandon Braden to the death the fates had assigned him, even to save her own hide. If the worst happened, she wanted to hold her love in her arms as he passed from this world into the next, and give him whatever comfort she could.

Just the thought filled her eyes with tears.

Braden saw her and pulled away from his circle of friends to greet her with a husbandly kiss on the forehead. With one hand he held her shoulder, with the thumb of the other, he brushed the wetness from her cheek.

"This day will pass, beloved," he told her quietly. "Tonight, you and I will celebrate my victory together."

Conscious of Alaric standing nearby, Frankie shivered. "Who is your opponent?"

Braden lowered his hands to his sides. "I don't know. Lots will be drawn before the competition begins." He offered her his arm as the trumpets sounded, evidently to mark the beginning of the first event. They were settled on a high wooden dais, in straight-back chairs, before he spoke to her again. "First, the joust."

Frankie sat stiffly, biting her lip, as men in heavy armor, mounted on spectacular horses, took their places at either end of the field. The tilt protected the animals to breast height, but the knights themselves were exposed to their onrushing opponent's lance.

Nothing in Frankie's high school performance of

Camelot had prepared her for the sight of two men riding toward each other at the top speed their burdened horses could manage, long spearlike weapons in hand. The sound was even worse, and she bit her lip throughout, and only kept her breakfast down by the greatest self-control.

The events seemed interminable, but finally, in midafternoon, Braden left the dais to take the field, wearing his sword and a chain-mail vest. Frankie wished he were in full armor or, better yet, that he'd been born in the right time period in the first place and avoided this moment forever.

The people cheered as he took his place in the center of the action and unsheathed his sword. Sunderlin ignored the adulation; his gaze locked with Frankie's, and he seemed to be making a silent promise that he wouldn't let anything separate them.

Frankie's vision blurred; she lifted her hand. *I love you,* she told him in the language of the heart. *Forever and always, no matter what happens, Braden Stuart-Ramsey, Duke of Sunderlin, my soul is mated to yours.*

Braden's opponent was a large man, not as solidly built but clearly strong. He had a red beard and a Nordic look and Frankie thought uneasily of the Viking god Thor.

She rose out of her chair when the blades were drawn, stepped off the dais, and moved through the crowd as the swords were struck together in a sort of warrior's salute.

The cheers and calls of the spectators seemed to Frankie to roll from some great, hollow cave, and the air pounded like a giant heartbeat. Over this, always, always, rang the cruel sound of steel on steel.

She might have stepped right onto the field if Gilford hadn't grabbed her and hauled her back against his rotund torso.

"Are you trying to get him killed?" the doctor rasped, his breath whistling past her ear. "Did you learn nothing before, when Sunderlin was wounded because of your recklessness?"

The thrumming in her ears stopped; suddenly everything was crystal clear. Something had passed between the warriors, and the crowd sensed the change and fell silent. The match had turned, between one moment and its successor, from sport to warfare.

Frankie almost screamed, so great and uncontrollable was her terror, but Gilford stopped her by pressing one meaty hand over her mouth and shaking her.

"You must not distract him!" he breathed.

Someone else did that, as it happened. Alaric rushed onto the field, shouting, and in that fragment of time Braden hesitated. It was enough for Thor, who plunged his sword straight into the Duke's abdomen.

Frankie felt the blow as surely as if it had been dealt to her. She shrieked in protest and furious grief, and somehow twisted free of Gilford's hold, stumbling as she raced onto the field and threw herself down beside Braden in the bloody dirt.

She was wailing softly, speaking senseless words, as she gathered him into her arms.

Remarkably he smiled at her, reached up to touch her face. "So you were right," he said softly. "It ends here. I'm sorry, my love, for not believing you."

Frankie sobbed when he closed his eyes, tried to shake him awake. It was no use, and she was like a wild creature when Gilford and another man took her arms and hauled her off Braden so he could be carried away.

The crowd had been stirred to rage by the spectacle, by the unthinkable fall of their legendary leader, but it wasn't Thor they turned upon.

No.

One of the women pointed at Frankie. "Witch," she said.

Others took up the cry. "Witch—witch—witch—"

"God in heaven," Gilford gasped, "it's happening. Come, Francesca, we must be away from here, quickly!"

Frankie was prostrate with grief; the damning words of the crowd meant nothing to her. She wanted only to sit with Braden, to tell him all the things she'd stored up in her heart, to hold his hand in case he would know somehow that she was there.

Alaric moved to join the others, who had encircled Frankie and the physician now.

"She knew this day would come," Braden's brother said clearly, gesturing toward Frankie. "She predicted it. Maybe she even made it happen with chants and magic!"

"Are you insane?" Gilford demanded of Alaric, holding tightly to Frankie, who was only half-conscious. He raised his voice, addressing the witch-hunters who surrounded them, looming closer and closer. "This is a mere woman, not a witch!" he cried. "She has a heart and soul, blood and breath, like any one of you!"

Frankie fainted at that point, only to revive a few moments later and find herself being forcefully separated from Gilford, her only defender.

"In the name of all that's holy," her friend begged,

his face wet with sweat and perhaps tears, "release her! She has done nothing wrong!"

"Silence!" Alaric shouted. "Why do you defend her, Gilford? Are you in league with this—this mistress of the devil?"

"You are a traitor!" Gilford accused in return. "Mark my words, Judas Iscariot, the Duke will avenge this wrong, and God Himself will come to his aid!"

Someone came forward from the seething crowd and struck Gilford hard with a staff. The big man's knees buckled and he went down, and the sight shook Frankie partially out of her stupor. At last she realized what was happening.

She was dragged, kicking and scratching, to the whipping post, a horror she had not seen before, and thrust against it with cruel force. Her arms were wrenched behind her and tightly tied with narrow strips that bit into the flesh of her wrists.

For a few moments Frankie honestly didn't care whether she lived or died. After all, Braden was dead—he'd perished in her arms. If there was an afterlife, she might see him there.

As the villagers began stacking twigs around her feet, however, and as their eyes filled with unfounded hatred, it occurred to Frankie that she might be carrying Braden's child. It didn't seem fair that the infant should die before living.

Frankie fought hysteria as she searched the mob for one friendly face, one person who might dare to speak for her. There was no sign of Gilford—he had been overcome and perhaps even arrested—but Alaric soon approached, as if drawn by her thoughts.

"I warned you, Francesca," he scolded. No one would ever have guessed from his manner that he'd just seen his only brother die, that he was about to watch another human being burned alive. "You should have listened to me. I would have taken you away."

"You did it on purpose," Frankie accused, as the terrible realization dawned. "You weren't going to help Braden on the field; you only wanted to distract him so that his opponent could run him through!"

Unbelievably, Alaric smiled. "You might have been my duchess, after a decent interval had passed," he said. "How sad that you would never listen to reason."

Frankie spat at him, though until then her mouth had felt painfully dry. "I'll burn for a few minutes," she hissed, causing the mob to gasp in fear and draw back, "but you, Alaric Stuart-Ramsey, will suffer the flames of eternity for what you've done! *You are cursed!*"

Alaric paled, then his jaw hardened. "Bring the torches!" he cried.

Frankie watched in stricken horror as the pitch-soaked torches were lit and then laid to the dry twigs at her feet. She heard the crackle of burning wood, smelled the acrid smoke, saw the shifting mirage of heat rising in front of her like a wall.

Then she heard Merlin's voice, though she could not see him.

"Think of Seattle, Francesca," he said urgently. "Think of the big white ferryboats crossing Puget Sound. Think of those wonderful snowcapped mountains, and the hillsides carpeted with green, green trees. Remember your shop, and your cousin Brian, and your friends. Remember the Space Needle, and Pioneer Square, and the Pike Place Market—"

Tears rolled down Frankie's cheeks as she tilted

her head back and remembered with all her might, with all her being. She felt the flames begin to catch at her skirts, felt the horrible, choking heat . . .

"Seattle," said Merlin. "Seattle, Seattle—"

"Witch!" screamed Alaric, his voice hoarse and fading. Slowly fading, into the heat, beyond it. *"Witch . . ."*

There was no explosion, no sprinkling of magic dust. The shift was graceful and quiet.

Frankie's first realization was that it was cooler, that her hands were no longer bound. She opened her eyes and found herself staring into a shop window at her own reflection.

She was wearing a silk dress, torn and singed, and her face and hair were dark with soot. Taxis and pedestrians moved past, also mirrored in the dusty glass, and Frankie turned slowly to look.

Pioneer Square.

Frankie began to weep, stumbling through staring, whispering tourists, street people, and office workers, making her way around the corner.

The sign above her shop still read CINDERELLA'S CLOSET. Frankie sagged against the door, sliding downward until she was sitting on the worn brick step.

Passersby stopped and made a semicircle around her; Mrs. Cullywater pushed through, carrying a bag from a nearby bakery in one hand and wearing the key to the shop on her wrist, dangling from a pink plastic bracelet.

"Why, Miss Whittier!" the friendly old woman cried, dropping the bag and crouching. "What's happened? Merciful heavens, how did your clothes get into such a state. . . ."

Frankie drew up her knees, wrapped her arms

around them, and shook her head from side to side, unable to offer a sensible explanation.

SHE spent that night in Harborview Hospital, under observation, but was released in the morning. A friend, Sheila Hendrix, brought jeans and a T-shirt and drove Frankie back to her apartment.

"I'll stay if you want," Sheila said. She was obviously worried, but Frankie didn't want to keep her. Sheila had a good job with a local advertising firm, and she had better things to do than play nursemaid.

"I'll be all right," Frankie insisted, and Sheila left.

The apartment was unchanged, except that everything was covered with a fine layer of dust and the plants were all desperate for water. Frankie made a ritual of small chores, but the place was small, only a studio, though it was attractive, and all too soon there was nothing to do.

Frankie sank onto her couch, gnawing at her lower lip. It was only a matter of time before the police would show up, wanting to know what she'd been doing, staggering through the streets in such a state, with her dress half burned off and her hair and face covered in soot. Given the bohemian nature of Pioneer Square, she could probably convince them that she'd been practicing to become a street performer.

What would be harder to explain, however, was her total lack of identification. Her passport, driver's license, and credit cards were all still in England, in the Grimsley Inn, where she'd left them before going to the medieval fair that first day.

She splayed her fingers and plunged them into her hair. Braden, she thought, with a sorrow so desperate, so all-encompassing, that it was crushing her.

Oh, Braden. What do I do now? How do I go on
without you?

Somehow, though it seemed an impossible thing
to do, Frankie did manage to go on with her life.
After a few days the police casually stopped by to
ask what had happened, why she'd been wandering
in the streets in a charred dress, and she told them
she was into performance art. She didn't think for a
moment that they believed her, but they had other
concerns and didn't press.

Mrs. Cullywater stayed on to help run the shop,
since Frankie was in a daze of grief most of the time,
and it was that kind woman who called the inn in
Grimsley and asked them to send back Miss Whittier's identification, along with her suitcase. Yes, the
older woman assured the clerk on the other end of
the line, Miss Whittier was fine. She'd left Great
Britain under special circumstances and apologized
sincerely for any concern her disappearance might
have caused.

A month had passed since her dramatic return
from England, and Frankie was sitting in her shop,
watching lovers pass by on the sidewalk, hand in
hand. She was sipping strong tea and feeling sorry
for herself when a terrible crash sounded from the
back of the shop.

Mrs. Cullywater, normally unflappable, was back
there sorting a shipment of antique buttons, and she
let out a scream that all but cracked the window
glass. Frankie spilled her tea and overturned her
stool in her haste to get to her employee.

The shop was small, and very narrow, and Frankie
had to make her way between counters of old jewelry, racks of both vintage and used designer cloth-

ing, and pyramids of hatboxes. When she burst into the storeroom, she screamed, too—not for fear, but for joy.

Braden was sitting on the floor, clad in his usual leggings and tunic, looking dazed and very pleased with himself. "God's knees," he said. "I finally managed it."

Mrs. Cullywater had collapsed into a chair and was fanning herself with an old copy of *Photoplay*. "Out of nowhere," she muttered. "I swear, he just appeared out of nowhere."

Frankie was kneeling on the floor, laughing and crying, fearing to close her eyes lest Braden disappear again. She flung her arms around him, held on tight, and sobbed because he was real, and because it was no dream.

"How—?" she finally managed to choke out. "Oh, Braden, I thought you were dead!"

He got to his feet, bringing Frankie with him. "Gilford was there to take care of me." Braden put his arms around her, held her loosely, so that he could look down into her eyes. "You should have heard the uproar, Duchess, after you disappeared right out of your bonds the way you did!"

Frankie reached up, tentatively touched Braden's face. "How did you get here?"

"Your wizard came to my room one night and told me to remember all the things you'd told me about your world. He said I might be able to get to you, since I was supposed to be born here in the first place. I failed any number of times, but I'm glad I kept trying."

Mrs. Cullywater edged around them and fled the shop. Frankie hoped the poor dear wasn't too frightened, but she did not go after the older woman. Any attempt to explain would, of course, have only made matters worse.

Braden bent his head, kissed Frankie lightly on the mouth, the way he always did before he made slow, sweet, thorough love to her. "For a time there," he confessed a moment later, "I thought the villagers might have been right about you. Who else but a witch could vanish the way you did? It was Gilford who set me straight and said you'd come back here."

Frankie remembered the insane anger of the mob and shivered, and Braden held her a little closer. "I thought they were going to kill him, too, because he tried so hard to save me."

Braden shook his head. "They gave him some bruises and scrapes, all right, but he was a healer. They needed him, and they knew it."

Frankie laughed, even though her eyes were glistening with tears. "How are we going to explain you to the modern world, Braden Stuart-Ramsey?"

He gathered her to him and kissed her in the way she'd dreamed of, remembered, mourned during the long weeks since their parting. "We'll worry about that later," he said. "For now, Duchess, I just want to hold you in my arms."

Not wanting to confront Braden with the strange sights and sounds of the nineteen nineties without some preparation, Frankie took him by the hand and led him through the alleyways to the rear entrance of her apartment building. They climbed the inside stairway and hurried along the hall to Frankie's door.

They were inside before Braden really began to absorb his surroundings. He touched the television set in curious bewilderment, and Frankie smiled. She would show him how it worked later; with the twentieth century rushing at him from every direction, his senses were surely approaching overload as it was.

"Where do you sleep?" Braden asked when he'd checked out the bathroom, where he immediately flushed the toilet, and given the kitchenette a quick examination.

Frankie was just standing there, leaning against the door and silently rejoicing. She was all but blinded by tears, and yet she couldn't stop smiling. That is, until she remembered that he'd suffered two grievous sword wounds in the space of a week.

She thrust herself away from the door and hurried over to him. "You're hurt—good heavens, in all the excitement, I'd forgotten—"

Quickly she removed the sofa cushions and folded out the hidden bed.

Braden stared for a moment, then crossed himself.

Frankie took his hand. "You need to lie down," she said.

He smiled. "What I need, Duchess, is for you to lie down with me." He pulled her close and kissed her in his old, knee-melting way. Gently he lifted her T-shirt off over her head and tossed it aside. "Strange clothes again," he teased, but he had no trouble removing her bra.

"Braden," she whimpered joyously as he cupped her breast in his hand, chafing a ready nipple with his thumb.

Sunderlin was fumbling with the snap on her jeans by then. "What manner of leggings are these?" he asked, but he didn't wait for an answer. Instead, he gently stripped away the last of Frankie's clothes and lowered her to the bed.

Frankie watched as her husband removed his own

garments, things that probably belonged in a British museum, and saw the scars on his belly and his right thigh. If anything, these imperfections made Braden even more magnificent. She held out her arms, and he fell to her with a low, hoarse groan of need.

"Your wounds?" Frankie asked, searching his eyes for some sign of the pain he had to be feeling.

Braden kissed her hungrily and at great length before answering. "My wounds will heal, now that I am with you again. For the moment, let there be no more talk of suffering, Francesca, or of trouble. We can think about our problems later."

Frankie arched her hips and deftly received him, delighting in the way he tilted his head back and moaned. "Much later," she agreed.

In that moment, somewhere far away and yet very nearby, a passageway between two eras closed without even a whisper of sound.